Stefan Prebil works and writes in his alpine cottage high above Lake Brienz.

After a career in top management around the globe, his work today consists of consulting companies on the technology sector, coaching and - in writing novels.

His stories deal with personal relationships, extraordinary biographies, in the context of social developments and rapid technological progress.

.

Stefan Prebil

Ramey Rieger

ICE DIAMONDS

VOLUME II

NOTHING IS ENOUGH FOR WHOM

ENOUGH IS TOO LITTLE

www.tredition.de

© 2020 Stefan Prebil

Cover, illustration: Stefan Prebil

Cover picture: Stefan Prebil

Translation and   Ramey Rieger
proofreading:

Publishing & Printing: tredition GmbH, Halenreie
40-44, 22359 Hamburg

ISBN
Paperback   978-3-347-03041-1
Hardcover   978-3-347-03042-8
e-Book   978-3-347-03043-5

Content

ONE

O "kay, Chuck. Man, it sure is good to hear your voice! We'll talk more when you're here. Send me an SMS when you know what time your train's getting in." Sam taps his phone to end the conversation and lays the device on the coffee table. Sliding open the terrace door, he lets his gaze wander over the lake. It's nearly summer. A late morning wind sweeps briskly through the valley, driven by hazy sunlight.

He's looking forward to seeing Chuck again. They had parted ways at Hallgrímskirkja, Iceland's mighty cathedral, the final bastion above the ruins of Reykjavik. The last Sam saw of him, Chuck was hobbling to rescue busses heading for Keflavik to search for his darling Seydür. Sam and the other diving guides, Marie, Piet, Jace, Emma and Barbu, escaped in a *borrowed* Cessna to the Faroe Islands.

Sam shakes his head, smiling. He may have once held a private pilot's license for single-motor aircraft, but he still can't believe he navigated a dual-engine plane through the hurtling magma of

Katla's eruption, landing them all safely in Vágar. It was a miracle. An absolute miracle.

Two days ago, their train finally pulled into Interlaken where they caught a taxi to Sam's small lakeside house. It had been no easy task getting from Tórshavn to Liverpool. The sea was full of fishing boats transporting refugees from Iceland to the Faroes and the ferries were packed with unscathed survivors. Overseas tourists hoped to find ships and trains in England to take them to their final destinations. After receiving their emergency passports, it took the friends another ten days to get seats on the ferry.

Barbu is probably still stranded on Stremoy, waiting for his papers to arrive from Romania. They had each given him fifty euros to tide him over as well as five of the obscure stones they had found during their trek through Icelandic fire and brimstone. Barbu had promised to get in touch as soon as he arrived at home.

In Liverpool, they put Jace on a train to London. He was carrying a few sample stones and photos of the entire collection. The plan was to show these to his cousin and have them assessed.

Once they had seen Jace off, Emma, Marie, Sam and Piet took a ferry to Brest. There, their odyssey to Switzerland began. With transport vouchers and limited funds, they were forced to take countless regional trains, sometimes waiting hours for a connecting train to take them one leg further south. A few hours short of three days, they arrived in Interlaken. Fortunately, they had thought to contact friends and family while at the b & b on Stremoy, promising to call when they arrived in Switzerland.

Finally, in Sam's hometown, they bought cellphones and Swiss SIM cards, a few clothes and plenty of food to stock the refrigerator. They will settle into Sam's house and wait for news from Jace. Their lives are on hold. Are they rich? Or just foolish?

Katla has spent the brunt of her fury, now spewing but a thin stream of ash into the sky. Yet between the two eruptions, first the volcanic system beneath Langjökull glacier, then Katla, masses of ash particles have been vomited into the stratosphere, circling the Earth several times. The entire Northern hemisphere's early summer sun is hidden behind grey shrouds. A November sky at the end of June, stretching as far south as Switzerland. It will be some time before civilian air traffic resumes.

Of course, the fates of Icelanders and tourists have the media's undivided attention. Reruns of pre-disaster Iceland documentaries were dusted off and aired between reports on rescue missions, international efforts and individual survivor portraits. The news programs broadcast countless expert prognoses on a looming economic crisis or, at least a severe recession triggered by the ash clouds. It was true that several major airlines have recently filed for bankruptcy. EU economic ministers have formed crisis committees and are meeting daily to forge plans to rescue the economic, agriculture and tourist industries, further burdening the overtaxed population for decades to come.

Despite it all, the people themselves have reinstated a kind of normalcy. Vacations in Thailand have been struck from the program and neighborliness is back in fashion. Food is shared, gatherings more frequent. Governments have ordered food rationing since the clouded sky hit in the middle of the growing season, stunting food production and limiting supply. For the most part, people are making the best of things. The rare cases of looting are nipped in the bud and chaos curbed. In the reigning atmosphere of generosity and solidarity, political parties smelling an opportunity to denounce the current system hold their tongues. They would only damage their own image.

Sam lights up a cigarillo and tries to recall exactly when he had packed his bags and left the house. The plan was to set out on a new life as a diving guide, leading tourists through the incomparably beautiful and unique Silfra Crack. He had been more than happy to mothball his tailored suits and silk ties and earn a fraction of his executive manager's salary. Was that a mere eight or nine weeks ago? So much has happened since then. It feels like years since he locked up and took a taxi to the airport, Iceland-bound.

He gazes sightlessly at the mountains flanking the other side of the lake. Few could understand how he could throw away his lucrative position for a youthful dream, living in a concrete dormitory with other guides half his age. He was fifty-five, for heaven's sake! Why didn't he just buy a Porsche and find himself some pretty young thing? Just one of the less than complimentary comments colleagues had made. But Sam knew his mind, always had. He loved a good risk, otherwise would never have made it from pharma-salesman to CEO.

It just felt right and once on Iceland, he had quickly adjusted to his new life, completely surrounded by pretty and handsome young things, none of whom had a Porsche and most of whom could have been his children. It was fantastic! Then he began a passionate affair with Marie, an incredibly sexy Frenchwoman, and ended up falling head over heels in love with her. Life was good! He was utterly in his element and had never felt so at home in his skin.

Iceland! This primal land of one hundred and eighty active volcanoes and six hundred minor earthquakes a week, found it was time to teach its people and more than a million tourists overrunning its rare and delicately balanced beauty a lesson in humility. Several volcanoes were over way due, but, Sam thought, couldn't they have waited just a little longer? He had literally just taken the dive into this life! Sam shakes his head. How arrogant can you get? He and his friends had had incredible luck to escape with their lives, not to mention the stones they had found. They might even be incredibly rich.

Frame by frame, Sam's mind replays the dread and terror: The slick and deadly lahar, triggered by eruption and earthquakes, avalanching down the glacier, amassing boulders, trees and blocks of ice as it gained velocity and mass before crashing into Silfra, obliterating its ethereal beauty; the seven of them like tiny ants in a ranger's jeep, desperately trying to outrace the avalanche and barely making it up the slope where an antenna mast saved them. And that's where Jace discovered the milky white stones they had stuffed into their pockets, believing they were raw diamonds. And where they lost Simi. They still don't know if the stones really are diamonds. Sam's inner film rolls on and he sees them standing there shocked and helpless as a tidal wave crashed into Reykjavik, wiping out the entire city. He sees them huddled together, slowly picking their way over mass destruction, then finding Marie and finally escaping in a Cessna some Swedish guy had readied for an afternoon jaunt. Sam still doesn't know if the plane's owner lives. They had been outrageously lucky.

Endless shudders run down Sam's back as the images march mercilessly through his mind. His belly tightens, his heart pounds and he's back in the midst of the nightmare.

So many people died. First Simi, in a frenzy at the prospect of wealth, chasing an over-sized stone to his death; Ian at Silfra, determined to save the ranger despite the lahar gaining momentum at his back; Mickey, buried together with his Julia in the seething waters of Lake Þingvallavatn as Sam watched him desperately trying to find her; and all the other teams and tourists who never had a chance to get out of Silfra in time; Ilias, the lonely Greek who died in the tidal wave. These were the dead he knew by name. There were tens of thousands others he didn't. Sam closes his burning eyes as if in doing so he could shut out the horror. He takes a deep and calming breath, consciously relaxing his muscles. He's alive! Marie, Jace, Emma, Chuck, Piet and Barbu! They all made it and that's what counts right now.

It seems Iceland was moving on in the same spirit, pulling themselves up and out of the rubble and grief, as they have been doing for generations on end. NATO troops organized multi-national fleets to evacuate survivors from the devastated island nation. Low-altitude military helicopters are transporting urgent cases directly to various British clinics. The severely but not life-threatening wounded distributed among the numerous hospital ships. Any non-native still standing is brought aboard ferries and NATO ships and initially taken to the Faeroe Islands. Embassies are overrun, processing the hundreds of stranded tourists. Icelanders gather in the warehouses, discussing possible futures, mourning their dead.

Sam presses his cigarillo against the railing to extinguish the ember and pockets the butt. Modest as it is, his domicile on Lake Brienz took them in, offering a great deal more comfort than V18. The spacious living room's double French doors lead onto a wooden terrace jutting out over the lake. Marie and Sam have taken up residence in his bedroom and Emma occupies the guest room. Piet set up camp in Sam's office where there is space enough for Chuck when he comes. Who knows when Barbu will arrive, but they'll find room for him, too.

Sam is leaning on the railing and looking out over the lake when Marie comes up from behind, slipping her arms around his chest. "Everything okay?" Sam gently removes her arms and turns to face her. "Imagine, Chuck called. He's on his way here and I'll pick him up tomorrow at the train station."

Before Marie can begin to ask the thousand questions springing to mind, they hear the front door open. Evidently, Piet and Emma are back from their trip to the supermarket. Marie kisses Sam on the lips, winks and calls out, "Hi guys, come on out, we've got some news!"

Piet fishes a couple of beer cans from the shopping bag and places them on the glass table. "Ice cold," he says with an impish grin. Emma brings a bottle of coke and two glasses from the kitchen. Her assumption that Marie isn't drinking beer at this early hour is correct. The four of them settle into the rattan chairs surrounding the table. The men drink deeply from their beers.

"Has anyone talked to Barbu?" Emma asks.

"No, but I got a call from Chuck today while you were shopping," Sam reports, looking at each of them in turn. "Evidently, he couldn't find Seydür. He looked everywhere for her. It's tragic! Either she is buried beneath the rubble or she made it to Keflavik. But she wasn't in Keflavik either. So, he assumes she found her way to relatives somewhere on the island. If she's still alive, that is."

"Oh my god!" Emma exclaims. "What a nightmare! How's he holding up?"

"Oh, he joked about it, said he was jilted at the altar without a word of explanation. But you know Chuck. I don't believe he's as tough as he makes out to be. I think he's hurting badly."

"How can you tell?" Emma asks.

"He kept changing the subject, didn't want to talk about it. When I asked him how he felt or how he was coping, he didn't really answer, just asked about the stones. Are we rich or not? That's all he wanted to know. Naturally, I told him Jace was going to his cousin, maybe he's already there, and we have to wait until we hear from him. That didn't seem to be any comfort and now Chuck's on his way here."

"What? Chuck's coming here?" Piet asks, putting his beer on the table, his confusion evident. "Doesn't he trust us? I mean, I'm not Chuck, but I would keep looking for my love until I had some kind of certainty."

Emma and Marie nod silently. It's good to know Chuck is still in one piece and they'll see him soon. But on the other hand, Chuck can be a sly dog when it comes to getting his way. If the stones really are valuable, he will immediately start pressuring them into decisive action, and by decisive action he means he will make the decisions. He can be very persuasive when he wants something. Up to this point, they have tip-toed around the issue, merely indulging private fantasies before falling asleep at night. They imagine it would be like winning the lottery, with a boatload of tax-free money all at once. But often their imaginations failed them, they just couldn't believe it could really happen. But, what if? And vague dreams of wealth and luxury float through their minds. What they could do with so much money! All the same, the numbers have not yet been drawn. Are they holding a winning ticket or a blank?

"I don't believe Chuck doesn't trust us. He's compensating. Somehow the idea of being rich might make up for his loss, it has to. And, being Chuck, when he grabs hold, he doesn't let go. He wants a plan and, of course, knows what's best for everyone. By the way, I did get an email from Barbu. He's finally made it as far as Vienna. That's really good news!"

"Okay, and what will we do when it turns out we're rich as Croesus?" Piet throws out cheerfully. "Heard anything from Jace, Emma?"

"Yeah. Jace is at his uncle's house in London and his cousin, John, is taking the stones to one of his partners tomorrow to assess their value."

"Okay. But didn't he say anything at all?" Piet wants to know.

"Not really. John is extremely cautious and wouldn't want to say anything decisive until he's consulted a colleague. He did say, though, that it's a highly unusual story. That's all Jace could get out of him."

"Hmmm," Piet rumbles, looking around at them.

"Well, why don't we play what if?" Marie says into the brooding silence. "What if we really are rich? What if we manage to sell the stones? I mean, what if we're super rich? Billionaires, if our calculations at Guðrun's were correct. What would each of us do?"

They exchange astonished glances. It's as if it is the first time, they have ever considered the idea. Of course, images of a carefree life have passed through their minds ever since they found the stones. But none of them have a truly concrete idea. The mere sum is unimaginable.

None of them, excepting perhaps Sam, has had experience with large amounts of money. And he's a newbie to wealth of this caliber, too.

Like the rest of humanity, there had been times when they had lost themselves in dreams of what if. Especially when money was tight, or desires far outreached their bank accounts. Idle daydreams staving off reality for a moment, like a large slug of whiskey to fog over vexation, allowing the alcohol to wrap you in a warm blanket against the cold, cruel world.

What if? A delightful bedtime story shutting out reality and allowing you to sleep easy; a fantasy of uncountable riches and the freedom they bring as well as the fulfillment of every material wish; a long, hot bath in security. You are rich.

At first – at least that's what people say who have experienced such wonders – there is a kind of numb incredulity. But once your brain surrenders to the impossible, pure joy sets in, blissful reality that you never believed would happen to you. Your thoughts begin to jostle for attention, trying to shout each other down, "WOW! I'll never have to slave at my job again. I can pay off all my debts. I'm FREE!!" And then, "Ten million, incredible. But wait, didn't someone win ninety million just couple of months ago? Shit, why do I have to win such a pittance? I mean, the odds of winning at all are astronomical. So what? Ten million is enough for a lifetime. I can buy whatever I want!" And then, "I hope taxes don't take a too big of a bite out of my pie!"

Thoughts ping-pong from misgivings to vexation to the thousand possibilities opening before you, including a new, sly fear of covetous friends and family. All this interwoven with joyful anticipation like a child on Christmas morning gaping at all the gifts beneath the tree, wondering which wishes on the list have come true.

What would be on Sam's list? On his colleagues' lists? A beautiful villa somewhere in the country. A mega-cool off-road ten-cylinder Mercedes. And of course, a convertible for the summer months. Oh, yes, the villa will need to have a pool. Travel! An Arctic expedition with diving excursions and then a safari tooling through Africa's savannah in the Mercedes. But why not a trip around the world? In a luxury catamaran rigged out with only the very best, sailing to all the best known and unknown diving spots. Diving, for sure! Maybe the best idea would be to open a diving base on an island with one or two speedboats, super-correct of course – sustainable, clean, exclusive. No more cheap tourist traps. But is ten million going to be enough? Damn! Why couldn't it be more? Enough for all this and a house for my mother, she's certainly earned it. A college education for my sister who is struggling to raise her kid alone. Ten million is not enough, I'll have to make choices, strike stuff from the list. So, what's new? Isn't that what I've been doing all my life?

And yet, their millionaire fantasies this time are only limited by the reach of their imaginations. This isn't a few lousy millions between them they're talking about, they're dreaming in the hundreds of million – for each of them.

The silence in the room is as deep as sleep, but their glittering open eyes tell of the castles each is building in his or her mind, from elegant country homes to golden palaces; from Lamborghinis to high-tuned Jeeps; from stud farms to diving resorts.

"So?" Marie asks, "What would you do with the money?"

Piet's voice is heavy with longing, "I would…"

"Hold your horses, my friends!" Sam interrupts him, "before we one-up each other with the most absurd ideas, we need to know the amounts we are working with and how we can turn the stones into hard cash," Sam muses. "That's not going to be easy. We can't simply walk into a jewelry store and ask the jeweler if he or she wants to buy one or more raw stones. If they're really that valuable, it's going to take time to find buyers. And we'll have to be extremely careful or we'll have the authorities and media on our tails asking many uncomfortable questions." His words brought them back to earth with a thud, you could almost hear the bubbles bursting in their minds.

"You're right, of course," Emma takes up the thread. "But assuming we manage to take those hurdles, I think we should set up a charity. There is so much poverty and misery in the world and we literally stumbled over the stones. We did nothing to earn them, they are a gift of sorts. We should spread the wealth around; we owe the world that much."

"Chuck will have a field day when he hears you say that. I'm sure there's nothing farther from his mind and I can even understand his point of view," Marie remarks. "So many stinking rich people were born into wealth. You think they're grateful? No way. Why don't they set up foundations?"

"But they do!" Sam interjects, "Look at Buffet, Zuckerberg, Gates and what's their names. They've all donated millions, if you can believe what the media says."

"Well, that's just it. Can you believe what the media says? They might look noble in the press, but has the world changed an iota for the better? Besides, that's a whole other ballpark. They're still swimming in money even if they set up a hundred charities!" Piet exclaims, working himself into a lather. "To hell with charity, I want to set up a really good diving center. Better yet, a global chain with ecological standards and prices affordable for your average middle class. Or I'll just buy out the whole Iceland Adventure company and turn it into a sustainable, environmentally friendly business. If there's money left over, maybe then I'll consider donating, but not sooner!"

"I can see it's not going to be easy," Sam puts in thoughtfully. "There are seven of us, well let's say six since we can certainly count Chuck out of the donation calculation. If each of us donates separately it won't be half as effective as setting up an endowment. We need to agree on how much we put into it. It's a very good idea."

"So, we have to decide how much each wants to donate and the rest we can do with as we please?" Marie reckons.

"Yes, I think that's the right thing to do and I'm pretty sure Jace thinks so too. But we also have to think of our families and friends. They should get a piece of the pie, too, for their projects and needs. They all could use a little more money," Emma says.

Piet bursts into laughter and goes inside for another beer, muttering loudly, "You're all off your nut!"

"It looks like the first decision is whether a percentage of the money goes to charitable causes or not. If we agree to donate, should we pool the funds? And which percentage do we keep? Good thing we have time to think about it, because we're going to be hard put to reach a consensus. Money does funny things to people. What do you think?" Sam directs his opinion to the two women.

"You can't be serious! Are you out of your minds? For once, life has sent some luck my way and I can do things I never even dared to dream of and the first thing you think of is the poor little children in Africa? Count me out! Cheers!" Piet calls angrily from the kitchen and they hear the hiss of a beer can opening.

They all tacitly agree to drop the subject.

"Men!" Marie exclaims, laying an arm around Emma's waist as they go out on the terrace.

Sam takes a deep breath and opts for drinking beer with Piet rather than wrestle words with the women.

"What's the point?" Piet grumbles angrily, taking a seat at the bar in the kitchen. "Do they seriously want to play Albert Schweizer and save the world from poverty? Utterly naïve women's talk!"

"Let it go, Piet. Don't count your chickens before they're hatched. I'm sure we'll each have enough to make ourselves a good life," Sam soothes, rubbing Piet's shoulder with one hand.

"I wonder," Piet rejoins, "What do you plan to do with your cut?"

"Hmm. Sure, I've given it some thought. I already have this house, a good car and enough to travel. Do I have to get a bigger one, better one, just because I can afford it? I'm happy enough to never *ever* have to take on some sickeningly boring and exhausting job just to pay the rent."

Piet nods thoughtfully. "But there must be something you would love to do with the money besides giving it away. I've got loads of ideas."

"I read a study once some institute made on people who have won the lottery. Ever heard of it? It must be something like falling in love. After a month or two on cloud nine, blissfully certain you've found your destiny, nearly every winner comes down to earth with a crash. Most go bankrupt and are more miserable than they were before they had won. I would hope we could be more prudent instead of throwing money around like star-struck teenagers."

"Maybe you're right," Piet concedes, "but my dreams have nothing to do with fat cars, luxury homes and such shit. Well, not exclusively. I'd be nice to be able to throw some cash out the window for once. But my real dream is to set up a world-wide network of diving resorts. Sustainable, with biologists who show guests how beautiful and fascinating the ocean and its inhabitants are, like Jacques Cousteau once did. He knew what he was talking about, he's my hero. Did you know he wanted to build an underwater city? I would start with an underwater resort. Maybe I can make that dream a reality now." Piet's eyes are glittering with boyish eagerness.

"Hey, that sounds really cool. I can easily imagine setting up a diving base. I even suggested it to Marie a few days ago," Sam replies.

While listening to Piet, he was struck with how few visions he has held onto from his youth. He realizes he had never been much for building castles in the air but a veritable master architect when it came to building castles in the sand. If he is honest with himself, he would gladly give away all his wealth, even sell his soul to the devil or whoever is in charge of such deals in exchange for an enduring love and partnership. Maybe even have children and spend his old age surrounded by caring family. The one thing he truly longed for could not be bought. Which is why he only dared to mention a diving base to Marie. Not because it really meant so much to him, but he believed it would appeal to her.

"Just this morning Marie told me I was just one more mindless loser in a diving community full of childish adventure-seekers who can't see further than their flippers. Finally, we hit it rich and the world is our oyster. But instead of coming up with something truly meaningful, all we can think about is a diving base. Seems she had you in mind," Piet throws out there, looking at his beer can as if it were a new discovery. He belches loudly.

"Hmm," Sam grunts, unwilling to take the bait but feels a knot gather in his gut.

"Emma stood by and nodded her applause. Apparently her Jace is also running on about the diving base idea. And these are the men they want to spend their lives with? Marie warned her off, saying there's no relying on men anyway.

When it comes down to the nitty gritty, they're no-where to be found or just do as they're told like good little boys. So, Emma shouldn't get her hopes up. Which category do you fall into Sam?" Piet asks with a crooked grin.

Sam blushes slightly but doesn't answer. It's a good question, though, which category? Probably the latter until his capacity for being good runs dry and he reverts to the former. At least that what his track record shows. Changing the subject, he asks Piet a question of his own, "Where would you set up your first diving base?"

"Iceland," Piet replies immediately, searching Sam's face for consternation. "They're finished for the moment, there's no competition. The state would jump for joy if I turned up shopping for a boatyard where I could build modules for my un-derwater hotel. Then, even people who don't dive could discover the underwater world and take an interest in saving the planet. That's a thousand times cleverer than this tree-hugging bullshit or saving the world with donations to cure poverty," Piet snorts, getting caught up in his dream.

"When did you talk to the two of them?" Sam wants to know, but Emma and Marie come in from the terrace arm in arm, laughing at some private joke.

Piet and Sam exchange a look. Enough for now. No reason to feed the fire and burn down the house before they have any cash in hand.

The women enter the kitchen and Sam smiles his most charming smile, "May I offer the ladies a beer?"

They both nod.

That night, lying in bed, Marie broaches the subject again. "Sam, chériee, what do you really think about all this? It just seems so ominous, these sudden riches and I'm afraid it's not going to be a joy ride. I don't even know if it's a good thing. I wish none of this had happened and I was still a poor diving guide on Iceland."

She slips out of his embrace and sits up in bed. Sam mumbles something incoherently.

"I can't sleep," Marie tries again. "Please, talk to me."

Sam pushes himself up with a grunt and sits next her, "There's no simple answer, Marie. There are a thousand thoughts running through my mind about our society, about our system and about my own values. When money comes into play, things get complicated. And even if I could come to some kind of conclusion, we still wouldn't know how to go about reconciling our various hopes and wants and become joint benefactors.

"Explique mois, explain! I want to know what you think, Sam!"

"I can try," Sam rumbles. Marie lays back down, pulling Sam next her and cuddling up to him, her head on his shoulder, as if preparing to hear an exciting bedtime story.

"Once upon a time," Sam begins, "there was a beautiful blue planet. And on this planet, there lived a very strange species called homo sapiens…" Marie neither smiles nor speaks, she merely looks at him expectantly. Sam looks at her and sighs. She wants what she wants.

"Okay, Marie, I'll do my best to set aside my cynicism and admittedly rather pessimistic view of the world."

"That sounds like a good place to begin, mon cher. I'm listening."

"Maybe we should begin by giving our possibilities a certain dimension. Let's say the stones actually are worth a billion dollars. I don't believe they're really that valuable and even if they are, turning them into cash will be a challenge in itself. But, okay, we have a billion dollars to work with. If we transfer the money into an endowment and invest it – not in just anything but invest it as ethically as we can – we would earn approximately five percent interest per annum. That's fifty million dollars a year that we would have to distribute among projects and other humanitarian causes. I don't doubt that we could do much good with such a sum, but change the world? Inspire a true transformation like some of us imagine? Hardly. On top of that, there's no way we will quickly agree on what to do and how to do it; in which projects we should invest or launch ourselves. But that's another issue altogether."

"But you said yourself that many wealthy people invest a goodly part of their fortune in endowments to make the world a better place. We could pool our resources with one or more of them and then the money will be worth more," Marie ponders, twirling Sam's chest hair around her fingers.

"Certainly, we could, and it would actually be more effective, but let me describe the state of things in our capitalistic system. Take Switzerland for example. About ten percent of the population controls around ninety percent of total capital. It's about the same in all so-called developed countries. According to recent estimations, the richest man in the world is worth one hundred and forty billion. From that angle, our fifty million, or hundred million when we spend it all over ten years, are nothing but a drop in the bucket. We will certainly be able to ease the suffering of some people, but we won't be able to change the system. And when the money's gone, we're back where we started from." Sam's lecture is spoken softly with a touch of sadness in his voice.

"And why do you think we can't change anything? Isn't transformation a human possibility, overcoming our greed and joining together to make the world a better place? We are intelligent enough! Can't we turn our energies toward cleaning up the environment instead of poisoning the oceans; toward treating each other with respect instead of toward modern slavery to produce cheap t-shirts?"

"We would need to reprogram our basic software, the primary survival strategies of the human brain."

"Oh chéri! Stop speaking in riddles," Marie giggles, pinching Sam's nipple.

"Ouch! Fine, I'll try to explain my point of view but it's just one way of seeing things. There are thousands of approaches, thoughts and theories. Much more intelligent people have been wracking their brains for an answer to these questions since the beginning of human existence. First of all, I agree with you wholeheartedly. If humanity doesn't get moving and change their ways, we will die out just like the Neandertals. One theory proposes they became extinct when the climate became colder and hunting more difficult. Homo sapiens had a capacity for cooperation and hunted larger herds in groups. The Neandertals could only handle one companion, two at the most and were incapable of building clans. So, the little guys simply starved because their brain's strategy couldn't learn and evolve fast enough to ensure their survival."

Marie's pointer fingers draw circles in the air as if turning cogs in a machine.

"What I mean to say is," Sam continues, "we've come full circle and are standing on the brink of extinction. Our hunger for money only expresses our hunger for power. Or our fear of death. Over the last millennia, it has been dominion over Nature that determined whether humanity would survive and procreate or not. The principle of cooperation rose no further in the hierarchy, it was applied to the division of labor, but not to the ruling class. Still, this brought us enormous developments. We survived so successfully, our basic strategy to become as powerful as possible, to amass as much as possible, was so effective, we basically out did ourselves. We conquered Nature, or so we thought and still think. Now, the repercussions of our strategy are catching up with us. Overpopulation, apathy and greed threaten to destroy our means of subsistence and the battle for what resources remain is literally a fight to the death. I don't believe humanity has the willpower to transform and adapt to a world that provides less and less while our numbers continue to increase. We created the situation but are unable to cope with it. We will die out or diminish drastically and the human drama will begin again. Maybe then, the world will be a better place, and humanity will find the balance you and Emma so desire."

Sam lifts his head a bit and looks down at Marie. Her eyes are closed, her breathing deep and regular. He grins. His bedtime stories are better than any sedative. It wouldn't be the first time his talk has put a woman to sleep. Sam gently strokes Marie's head and lets his mind wander. Maybe Marie and Emma are right and he's just an old cynic. There are certainly indications that greed as a survival method has begun to transform. Baby steps, but possible to take. Change can happen, if each person starts with themselves.

For them, the true challenge will be agreeing on how to spend their fortune – if there's a fortune to spend. Still no word from Jace and he's been at his cousin's at least two days now. Maybe there'll only be enough to open up their own diving shop. That wouldn't be so bad and much simpler. Or would it? Hard to say. They are a pack of alpha wolves, not a beta among them. Sam has his doubts about their and his own ability to compromise, especially for the long term, when the dust has settled and routine returns. No matter how valuable the stones are, the danger of ugly confrontations is very real once they tap the root of all evil. Time will tell. Sam feels they are on the verge of something none of them could imagine and for which none of them, excepting perhaps Sam himself, are equipped. Just a week or two ago, they were tightly bonded within their shared passion for diving and the simplicity of life in V18. Now, they are faced with challenges and problems and probably nasty disputes, all of which they would never have if it hadn't been for Katla's eruption and the milky stones hidden beneath the Earth's crust.

TWO

Sitting in his car on the train station parking lot, Sam has the window down and is smoking a cigarillo to pass the time until Chuck's train arrives. It won't be long now. He charged the car's battery that morning to bring his old blue jeep back to life. Back in fashion, the jeep might be mega-cool, but like Sam, it's no spring chicken. Old, rickety, but still willing and able Sam thought with a grin as the motor finally coughed, shuddered and then roared to life. Sam patted the dashboard to express his solidarity.

After breakfast, Emma received a call from Jace. He told them he intended to come to Switzerland with his cousin John and that they will head for Zurich. Emma turned on the speaker so they could all follow the conversation. There was really only one question, but Jace wouldn't satisfy them. He must meet with John's contact first, but he would tell them one thing: they are not poor anymore. Whatever that's supposed to mean!

Sam empties his lungs into the misty sky. Ash particles are still veiling the sun, but it's not as bad as they said it would be a few days ago. Rainfall over much of Northern Europe has washed the air.

Now that the rainclouds have emptied their load, entire regions look like the aftermath of a garden bonfire. Houses, trees, streets, everything is blanketed with grey ash. Word has it though, that the jet stream is blowing hard northwards, sending the ash to the North Pole where grey polar bears blend in with a grey landscape.

Katla is still pouring lava over Iceland and spewing ash mile-high, but she's calmed visibly. Still, she could remain active for weeks or days, it's anybody's guess. Air Traffic Control has decided on opening air space under a twenty-four-hour stipulation as long as the wind doesn't change, and ash doesn't block air lanes. Hat's off to safety measures, but six airlines have already filed for bankruptcy and if the ban isn't lifted soon, the rest will follow in a few weeks.

If all goes well, Jace and John will take one of the first flights out of London for Zurich. If not, they'll take the train, arriving in two days instead of a couple of hours. Then, they'll finally know how much the stones are worth.

A whistle blast echoes over the platform and the inner-city train rolls into Interlaken station, warning away those who, as always, insist on standing on the edge of the platform.

Train doors open with a hiss and Chuck jumps onto the platform, a sea sack thrown over his shoulder. The first to debark, of course. Behind Chuck an elderly man helps a young mother lift her baby buggy out of the train. Sam shakes his head, grinning.

"Welcome, brother," Sam grunts and clasps Chuck in a bear hug. The hug is heartily reciprocated. They hold the embrace, clapping one another on the back. For a moment, Sam is overcome with all they had been through together and he feels a lump forming in his throat.

"You're looking old, man," Chuck remarks and releases his braying laugh. To prove him wrong, Sam slings the green sack over his shoulder and pulls Chuck by the arm to the jeep waiting behind the station.

"Let's get a drink before we go to your place," Chuck suggests once his sack is in the back and Sam opens the door. Sam frowns slightly and poses a silent question with his eyes, to which Chuck gives no answer. So, he locks the car and points his chin to the kebab stand across the street, its bleached plastic tables and chairs abandoned. Without a word they make for the stand and with beer in hand, seat themselves on the shabby chairs. The train station is nearly deserted. The usual herd of chattering Asians have stayed home this summer. At least thus far.

"Did you find Seydür? How is she?" Sam begins, understanding that this is a conversation Chuck would rather not have the others hear.

"No, I didn't find her, but I met a man who knows her. He told me she took a bus to the west of the island where her parents have a farm. I tried and tried to call but couldn't get through. I guess she's all right there. As you know, the clouds blew southwest in the beginning. But the wind has changed since then."

"You must be worried. How are you holding up?"

"Hmm, the first few days I was a mess. But now I think she's probably forgotten me. Just like a woman," Chuck says, giving an unconvincing laugh.

"I'm sure she'll call as soon as she can," Sam offers, knowing that Chuck has a new cellphone with a new number. But maybe they exchanged email addresses while they had the chance.

"We shall see," Chuck waves his hand as if chasing away a pesky insect, making it clear the love of his life is an irrelevant topic. "What's more important, I talked to Jace this morning."

"You talked to Jace this morning? We did, too. He's on his way to Zurich."

"Then you know we're loaded and will be swimming in money in couple of days."

"No, I don't...," Sam replies hesitantly.

"I know, that's why I want to talk to you. It's not that I don't trust the others, but It's obvious that you and I are the only ones who can handle this without doing something stupid."

Sam's eyebrows hit his forehead. What is he up to, this English bulldog looking at him with blood-shot, earnest eyes?

"I talked to Jace before he spoke to you all and convinced him not to say anything yet until I talked to you. So only the three of us know."

"Only the three of us? You mean, you've split us into two groups now? You, Jace and I against Emma, Marie, Piet and Barbu? What the hell?" Sam exclaims, suddenly feeling the weight of his bones succumbing to an unexpected, internal gravity.

"Hear me out first, then maybe you'll catch my meaning. If you don't agree, you can tell the others, okay?" The two men lock eyes. Chuck's gaze is clear and direct. Sam searches for some sly glint or greedy shadow but finds none. His expression softens and he prepares to listen impartially to what Chuck has on his mind.

"Let me begin at the beginning," Chuck launches his speech, shaking his head in amusement over Sam's misguided loyalty. What a bunch of pussies! Who cares if someone feels excluded? The main thing is not to make any mistakes! Just get the money! He thought Sam had more balls, never really believed his drop-out story, he was too educated, too world-wise. Only a few days after Sam turned up at Scuba Iceland, Chuck had researched him and knew exactly who Samuel Frei is but kept the information to himself. Knowledge is power.

"We have a total of six hundred, fifty-eight stones, two of them over five thousand carats, seventeen over a thousand, two hundred fifty over five hundred and the rest of them between fifty and two hundred carats," Chuck takes a breath.

We know that, Sam thinks and nods for Chuck to continue.

"They are all really big stones, even the smallest, not to mention the two mega rocks. Imagine!" Chuck goes on, waiting for some reaction but Sam only looks at him expectantly.

"In short, when all the stones come even close to the quality and purity of the sample stones Jace took to John for assessment, then…"

"Then?" Sam asks, his interest finally aroused.

"Then the rocks are worth about three billion…U.S. dollars, that is," Chuck whispers hoarsely. And there's the greed, that sly glint! Sam believes he is seeing a New Year's firework going off in his friend's eyes. His aching bones flare up, gather strength and drive into his belly. It's as if Chuck has just rammed his fist into Sam's gut. His legs go limp and he holds himself upright with the grimy chair's armrests. Chuck leans in close, his face no more than three centimeters from Sam's.

"Do you understand what I'm talking about now?" He breathes softly, clapping his palm around Sam's neck and holding him there a moment before sitting back in his chair, fishing out his cigarettes and lighting up, taking a deep pull. Chuck exhales forcefully, following the flight of two seagulls as they silently circle the train station before flying into the wind toward the nearby Aare River.

"Slow down. We don't have the money yet. All we have a is a bag of rocks," Sam says coolly. He breathes deeply and slowly, unclenching his stomach. Breathing is the key to keeping a clear head, not only true underwater.

"Exactly, my friend...and that's a critical point. John pulled some strings in London and was advised not to sell the stones on the open market or placing them on the diamond exchange. Too many people would get curious and Iceland might even claim the stones belong to them and not to us. Catch my drift?"

Sam nods, his stomach starts acting up again.

"Why do you think Jace and John are heading toward Zurich and not Amsterdam, the largest diamond market in the world?" Chuck waits.

"Because they can't sell the stones there," Sam replies.

"Precisely! But they can sell them in Zurich where there are highly confidential banks you can trace back to the tycoon Oppenheimer and the Jewish diamond syndicate. Today, they specialize in money-laundering and tax fraud, and you want to know how? With diamonds! The banks are still run by Oppenheimer's progeny. And even though the Indian and African syndicates in Holland control the world diamond market, it's the Swiss who ensure diamond prices stay high. Even if diamonds were no more valuable than copper, the Swiss would ensure they continued to be mined. To get to the point, John knows a very discreet syndicate member and contacted him from London. When the dealer heard the story, he invited the two of them to Zurich for an offer they can't refuse!" Chuck slaps his thigh enthusiastically, the hunger in his eyes a veritable blaze.

Sam is less than enthusiastic. He's worried, taking a sweeping view of their surroundings. No one is paying them any attention. But really, who would think the two men sitting in shoddy plastic chairs, dressed in threadbare jeans and jackets are talking about a transaction running to several billions of dollars? Now it's Sam's turn to search the sky for seagulls over the river. He has been around, seen a lot and is not very easily unsettled, but what he just heard shook him to the bone. The danger they are in hits him like a thunderbolt. They might not be running from a mud avalanche, but the hornet's nest they are stirring up could be just as deadly. They are meddling with powers far beyond their ken and tampering with the fortunes of the mighty is risky business indeed. Avarice is an extremely volatile monster easily aroused. Not only would they lose the stones, they would lose their lives.

Sam whistles softly through his teeth, "What's the plan?

"C'mon you idiot, a little enthusiasm please! We're rich! Okay, I know we have to keep our heads on straight and that's exactly why I don't want the women to know about it."

"And Piet..." Sam adds.

"Yeah, and Piet. Look, the plan's very simple. First, we find out how much the stones are worth, which means each has to be assessed individually. Then John can negotiate with the syndicate, maybe suggest a flat rate for the whole lot. A billion would be excellent, or maybe one and a half? We should at least get half of their total value. So, right now we can only wait until John and Jace meet this Arik what's-his-name and we have a clear sum to work with. Then we can tell the others. That way Jace can't call up his girlfriend, who is sure to tell Marie, and spill the beans."

Sam laughs out loud, shaking his head in astonishment. What a throwback! He wonders what made Chuck such an impossible chauvinist. But there's no denying his street smarts. He has an excellent antenna for looming danger and a knack for out-maneuvering his opponents. Chuck is certainly no coward, knows how to play his hand and can bluff to freeze your blood.

"Okay, we wait. They're meeting tomorrow, you say? Then we'll know soon enough. But either you or Jace confess to the women and Piet, I'd rather keep everything out in the open, it's easier," Sam remarks.

Chuck stands up, pressing his beer can flat with his weight. He places a hand on Sam's shoulder. "Good. Now you can drive me to your soon to be no longer humble home, Sam," he says with a chuckle.

Fifteen minutes later, the five of them are gathered around the table on the terrace. In honor of their reunion, Emma has prepared spaghetti vongole, Chuck's favorite dish. Marie and Emma bombard Chuck with questions about conditions on Iceland, how he managed to get to Switzerland and of course, whether, he had found Seydür and how she was, if he had. Piet watches Chuck and has a sneaking suspicion that something's not quite right. Chuck is unusually cheerful, open and warm – completely out of character and rather suspicious, Piet is sure of it but holds his tongue.

For the hundredth time they recount their flight from Silfra, Chuck's hair-raising sprint against the avalanche in the Land Rover and the antenna mast that saved them only to lose Simi as a result. They recount the tragedy and the horror they found in Reykjavik.

"Here's a toast to our reunion, to Barbu and Simi," Sam proposes, aiming to put an end to the endless replay of sadness they could do nothing to change. Chuck stands up and they all rise from their wicker chairs. They raise their glasses and Chuck pronounces, "To Barbu and Simi!"

"To Barbu and Simi!" they echo. As they raise their glasses to their lips, Emma's cellphone beeps. She pulls her device from her pocket and takes the call.

"JACE," she mouths. Her eyes light up and she smiles from ear to ear. She's missing him terribly, has heard from him only once and that was nothing personal, just business. It's so good to hear his voice! The others feel smiles forming on their faces as they watch her.

All at once, Emma's face is drained of all color, as if someone suddenly pulled the plug on her blood supply. She nods as if Jace could see her, "Okay, darling, please called me the moment you know more. Yes, I understand, please be careful, please. Yes, I love you, too."

Glasses in hand, they stand as if posing for an oil painting. Chuck is the first to break the silence, "What?"

"John has been kidnapped. He didn't return from a meeting with a syndicate middleman. Jace got an anonymous call and they told him nothing will happen to John as long as Jace follows instructions. They will call again as soon as Jace is in Zurich. They're watching him"

THREE

They slept little, discussing what to do as the night passed into a pale dawn. Forgotten were ideas about how to make the world a better place and what to do with so much money. Their talk wove in and out of their options and how, and if, they could salvage a small portion of the wealth attached to the stones. Of course, Chuck disagreed. He insisted that John's kidnapping was certainly a set-back and must be taken seriously, but, even though it sounds macabre, it could also be the fastest way to get the money. His matter-of-fact manner set their mind merry-go-rounds bouncing off in yet another direction.

Sam and Piet are certain that the syndicate is well-informed and knows exactly who they all are. They've probably even tracked down Barbu in Romania and none of them would have a moment's peace until the issue is resolved. Emma and Marie flared up at Chuck. The only important thing is getting out of the mess in one piece. All of them. To hell with the money. Rich but dead is not an option.

Breakfast is a brooding and silent affair that carried into the afternoon as they wait for Jace to call.

An eternity later, as they're gathered in the living room, five exiles on the same island, Emma's cellphone rings. Emma turns on the speaker and answers the call.

"Hi all, I've arrived in Zurich and have been waiting here at the train station for over an hour," Jace reports flatly. "No news. Either they don't know my exact arrival time or there's been a hitch in the program."

Now Sam's mobile chirps. Emma places her hand over her cellphone and Sam takes the call.

"Mr. Frei?"

"Yes, who's speaking?"

"Let that be our concern," a friendly voice states on the other end. "Your concern is to ensure we return John to you unharmed, which is also in our interest."

"Fine, what should we do?" Sam tries to match the casualness in the caller's tone.

"It's quite easy, Mr. Frei. Put all the stones into one bag and come to Zurich. We will call you with an address, to which you will naturally come alone. We receive the bag; you receive John and take the next taxi to a destination of your choice. Quite simple, isn't it?"

"Yes, that it is."

"And oh, Mr. Frei, please don't get the impression we are merely greedy thugs. Your John will be bringing his own bag in which you will find ten million dollars. Let's call it a sales transaction. There is, however, a small catch to the deal: You and your friends are never to speak of these events as long as you live. Be happy with what you get. And please take warning, we have eyes and ears everywhere. I don't believe we need mention what could happen if word got out, do we? But we are gentlemen, Mr. Frei, and our word is our bond. We are not fond of bloody messes."

Sam nods.

"Do you understand me, Mr. Frei?" The voice asks, unable to see Sam's nod.

"Certainly, I will discuss it with my colleagues."

"Excuse me, Mr. Frei, but I believe there has been a misunderstanding. There is nothing to discuss. You should merely inform Emma, Marie, Piet and Chuck. We'll be happy to inform Mr. Barbu via our Bucharest contacts, if you should so desire."

Sam swallows hard, his mouth is dry as dust. This is serious. He's familiar with his adversary's style, threatening in the kindest of voices with an elegant vocabulary. A very Russian way of doing business, as he recalls. The thugs were never the real threat. They would merely rip off your head and play soccer with it. The real danger lies with gallant bosses, who tenderly inform you where, when and why they have your entire family and friends in the crosshairs, mentioning your child's pet name and your wife's eye color. Tactful omniscience, leaving not the slightest doubt as to the extent of their reach and willingness to do harm. Sam remembers with a shudder how the police found an irascible businessman frozen in his rental car. The poor man had had too much to drink, lost control of his car at twenty degrees below zero. A sad, but common fate.

Sam is well aware of what this man, maybe it's Arik himself, is capable of despite his formal, courteous speech. He wants what he wants and intends to get it. Either according to his rules, without pain to life and limb, or otherwise.

"I see. Yes, now I understand you completely."

"Excellent! Be sure you are in Zurich by eight pm this evening. We'll be in touch and please don't forget to bring the stones, Mr. Frei. That would be a fatal error."

The line clicked and the busy tone peeped from Sam's mobile. His display announced an anonymous call.

Emma still has Jace on the line. They are all staring at Sam and the phone in his hand. Was it coincidence that they called just as when they were talking to Jace? And how did they get his number and all of their names so quickly? John must have talked. He would have, too, with wife and children at home, Sam thinks.

"What is it chérie?" Marie asks gently. Sam is as pale as the moon.

Sam reiterates the conversation word for word since they only caught his side. Jace is listening in and says, "I'll be on the next train to Interlaken and should be there in less than two hours."

"Okay, do that. We have about five hours until I have to catch the train to Zurich. If I catch the train," Sam replies.

"What are you talking about?" Jace shouts into the phone. Emma turns off the speaker and leaves the room, taking the terrace stairs to the narrow path around the house. She soon returns, mobile in hand. She walks through the living room and out on the terrace, gazing emptily over the lake, blind to her friends gathered around her, blind to the snow-capped mountain in the distance. Her lips are trembling.

"Is Jace okay?" Sam asks, stepping up to her and placing his hand on her shoulder.

"Well, sort of. He calmed down a bit. He feels responsible for what happened, for getting John into this mess. They are very close. Jace is godfather to John's youngest daughter."

Sam makes soothing sounds and strokes her back.

"What a nightmare this is!" Emma cries and turns her back on them. Marie, Piet and Chuck rise from their seats and take a step toward Emma. Even Chuck is touched and manages to keep his mouth shut.

Marie takes Emma in her arms and presses her close. Emma begins to quiver and her cellphone clatters onto the terrace boards. The three men stand about helplessly until Sam moves in and wraps his arms around the two women. Emma is sobbing quietly, as Marie gently strokes her hair. Piet overcomes his hesitation and brings what comfort he has in his arms to the group. Chuck feels like a fifth wheel and keeps his distance.

After while he reminds them, "Time's a-wast-ing."

"You're right," Emma concedes, unweaving their embrace, "We need a plan!" she says reso-lutely, walks back into the living room and takes a seat on the settee. They all follow her lead.

"What do you mean, a plan?" Marie asks. "The instructions and threats are both clear as Silfra," she adds, taking the place next to Emma.

"Emma's right…there are several points to con-sider," Chuck interjects, sitting down in one of the easy chairs while Sam and Piet occupy the sofa. "No question, our top priority is to have Jace back with us and John safely out of the syndicate's clutches, but…" and waits to see if one of them takes the bait. They merely look at him expect-antly and he continues, "But there are other things to think about as well. Do we really want to give up our treasure for a pittance? How much do they really know about us and about the stones? If we give them the stones, will that be the end of it, or will they chase us down anyway? And then, last but not least, do we really want Sam to drive down there alone? What if they just take the stones? No John; no money? What if they rip us off?"

"You call ten million a pittance? That's more than all of us combined could earn in a lifetime!" Emma exclaims angrily.

"You're right Emma," Sam agrees, adding, "but Chuck has a point, too."

"Yeah! So, what's the plan? Are we going to double deal the bastards and rescue John? Jace is fine," Piet declares heatedly, his face flushed.

"Easy, easy!" Sam interjects, his hands raised placatingly. "We all agree that John and Jace's safety is our uppermost concern – we don't really know what we're up against."

Emma and Marie exhale in relief when the other two men nod their consent.

"Chuck is right about one thing, though. If I go alone, we risk losing everything should they choose to cheat us. Chuck should hover in the background with the stones until we have John and know that Jace is safe. If something goes wrong at the transfer, well, that would be terrible, but not fatal," Sam suggests.

"Good plan," Emma says. "I don't really care about the stones and the money; I just want us all to be safe and able to carry on with our lives. Didn't we have enough nightmares on Iceland? The eruption and disaster were bad enough. We should really start to think about where we go from here, don't you think? Where and how we're going to live." She looks at each them in turn. Marie is definitely on her side.

"Exactly! And what we're going to live on plays a mighty big role in that theater," Chuck throws in with his braying laugh. Piet nods his agreement. The two men and two women try to stare each other down.

"Hmm, now that we've cleared that up, we have to decide whether we want to give the syndicate the stones for ten million or not," Sam put out there.

"What do you mean, whether? That's the only way to get John back, you mercenary bastards!" Emma shouts, shaking her head wildly.

"Take it easy, Emma. I ensure you that John and Jace's safety come first, I promise. But the syndicate most likely has no idea how many stones there are. You're both right, you know. It's true, ten million is a huge amount of money for us, but it's also true that they are taking advantage of our ignorance and are intent on only paying a fraction of what the stones are really worth. They know that we haven't the slightest idea; neither of their value nor how to sell them, although John probably does. That's certainly something to consider," Sam puts forward.

"Now there's an idea!" Piet proposes, clapping his hands. "We only give them half or less! That should do it!"

Marie is doubtful. "That`s taking an enormous risk. How do we know what they know?"

Emma can't stop shaking her head, disgusted with all of their grotesque deliberations.

"We don't, of course. But it would surprise me if John had shown them everything. Sure, he had the table listing all of the stones, their sizes and weights, but he only had a few pictures and a selection of the various sizes. He knows his way around, so why would he reveal the entire lot?" Sam replies smoothly.

"I can't believe you people!" Emma shouts, her face livid. "When did you get so calculating? Only yesterday we were fighting over what to do with the money! Now, you're all sitting around with dollar signs in your eyes and have gone utterly mad! You act as if you already have a fistful of dollars and to hell with John's life!" She jumps from the sofa in wrath and storms out of the house. Marie begins to rise and follow.

"Let her be, Marie," Sam advises. "She's justifiably upset. But right now, we need to think things through and make a sensible plan."

"Okay, lady and gentlemen, here's my suggestion: We pack both big guys, all the mid-sized and a few smaller ones in a bag for the drop. Why? Because we will still have nearly all small stones and they will be easier to sell. We'll have the ten million from the syndicate and enough stones to add to the kitty. And, if John hasn't said anything, we're the only ones who know where we found the stones," Chuck grins broadly at his own genius.

"Why the big ones?" Piet wonders, frowning "they're the most valuable!"

"It's a good idea," Sam concedes. "We'd have to cut the larger stones down to be able to sell them at all, and the middle ones raise the same problem," this to Piet. Sam looks at Marie for her opinion.

"Sounds plausible, but still risky. What will you do if they examine the stones before you have John and the money?" Marie asks, fretting her lower lip.

"Good point, darling. Chuck will hide in the car and wait for my sign before coming with the stones for the transfer. If they notice something's fishy, we'll have the rest of the stones in the car in a separate bag."

"Deal?" Chuck asks.

"Deal," Sam and Marie agree together.

"I still think it's bad business. We shouldn't give them so many stones in the first place," Piet objects.

Marie hears a sound and looks over to the door. Emma is standing there, rubbing her arm up and down in agitation. She had been listening and her eyes are ablaze. "Listen up, you idiots!" She hisses, "I'm going to the police. Now. Jace and his cousin are in the hands of gangsters and I'm not going to sit around and watch while you money-lusting trolls play games and endanger their lives!" Tears of rage and fear are in her eyes.

"And just what are you going to tell the cops, honey-buns?" Chuck asks angrily. "When they show up at the transfer and arrest the messengers, you can be sure you'll never see your boyfriend and his cousin again. Even if the police wait until John and Jace are safe, we will never be able to sleep in peace. Your parents or someone else in our families are likely to have an accident in the very near future. We would have no money, no stones and they will knock us off, one at a time." Chuck is nearly frothing at the mouth.

"Enough!" Sam cuts in sharply, jumping from his seat and spreading his arms commandingly.

Silence fell hard and complete, the air vibrating with tension. Chuck glares at Emma like a tiger ready to pounce and Piet stares at her in dismay. He draws breath to say something but Sam cuts him off, "That's enough! We should be looking for solutions, not at each other's throats!" He stands like a lion tamer, ready to crack the whip at the slightest misstep. Emma approaches cautiously, placing a placating hand on his outstretched arm.

Swallowing hard, but her voice steady, "Deal. But if anything should happen to Jace or John, I'll castrate the lot of you – for starters. You can bet your life on it!"

Piet admits defeat and raises his hand to high-five, each of them in turn. Chuck brays, looking at Emma, "Good girl."

Sam comes out of the bathroom with a large towel wrapped around his hips and pads to his bedroom. He feels much better after the ice-cold shower. The tension has left his body and the tingling reminds him of whose skin he's in. The chaos in his mind has come to order. He's glad they could come to an agreement on the next course of action, but he is fully aware of how precarious the current peace is. The flame of varying interests and needs are smoldering within their so diverse hearts. The smallest kindling could cause a bonfire. He hasn't the slightest doubt about that.

Before he slipped into the shower, Marie had caught him up in a warm and heartfelt hug. He felt this was her answer to the questions between them. Questions on what to do with the money, doubts about their differing ideas and fears as heated discussions rose among them all.

He feels ready now to face the transfer. He and Cuck will be leaving within the hour. Maybe he should lay down a while and gather his thoughts. He turns the knob on his bedroom door and steps inside. Just as he passes the threshold, two warm hands wrap around him from behind. Sam grabs them and spins around.

"Ouch! You're hurting me!" Marie whispers in surprise. Sam relaxes, also surprised at his reaction. Apparently, his subconscious is ready for fight or flight.

"Oh, Marie, I'm sorry…"

She stops his words with her lips, kissing him passionately, demandingly, yet Sam feels a tinge of desperation, too.

"You have to come back, do you hear?" she murmurs.

"Of course, I'll come back. Why shouldn't I?"

"Promise me!" Marie insists.

He gently strokes her soft hair and looks into her eyes, understanding her earnest need. He falls, as he does each time his eyes meet hers, and nods.

"Say it. I want to hear the words."

"I swear to you, my dearest darling, that I will return to your arms," Sam promises with a smile.

He can say no more. Marie sweeps the towel from his waist and pushes him onto the bed. He watches as she slips the straps from her dress over her shoulders, her eyes locked on his crotch, gleaming coquettishly. He follows her look. Not much happening down there. What does she expect? He has other things on his mind. Sure, the kiss was nice, but did not penetrate the current preoccupation.

"Marie, I have to get dressed, we need to leave soon," Sam protests.

"Shh, my darling, be still," she whispers like a mother soothing an anxious child. She sinks to her knees in front of him, kissing his thighs. Higher and higher, her mouth moves from one side to the other, gently biting, pressing her lips deeply into his flesh. Sam feels blood rushing to his loins when Marie raises her head and looks him in the eye. She opens her mouth slightly and moistens her lips with her tongue.

"Voilà! Now you're ready. You can get dressed now," she laughs, jumping up and falling next to him on the bed.

Sam turns his head and looks at her, taken aback. The look on his face is hilarious and Marie giggles behind her hand. Sam springs up in one motion and straddles her, grabbing her hands and pressing her arms over her head onto the mattress. His hips fall lightly onto her belly. She can feel his erection pulsating on her tense muscles.

"Oh yes, my darling, I'm ready. Can you feel that? I'm ready, but not to get dressed."

Marie flings her legs around his back, locking her ankles and pulling him closer. She bites him in the shoulder and neck, hard. What has gotten into her? Sam wonders for a second.

"I want you, chérie," Marie answers his unspoken question. "I want all of you, body and soul, heart and mind," she whispers in his ear.

Sam is suddenly overwhelmed, washed in warmth and comfort, safety and surety in the midst of all the chaos and trouble they have now and endured over the last weeks. He is home. Marie is his home and he never wants to leave her again. Body and soul, heart and mind, she said. The answer he has been waiting to hear to the question never asked, but there since the first time he held a woman in his arms.

Slowly and fully, Sam penetrates the woman of his dreams. She holds him tightly with her legs, allowing little movement, setting their rhythm with her hips. Each thrust is coupled with a question in her eyes, as if she is searching for an answer in the depths of his own. A question she also does not ask outright.

Desire flows through Sam's body, lapping into each cell, rising like waves out at sea gathering momentum. He sees Marie find answers in his eyes and her legs release him. She nudges him and they roll so she is now on top of him.

She needs to be in control. Is this what she seeks? Is she fearful of surrendering? Where are the roots of such fear embedded? What is this flash of anxiety that passes through her eyes when they are as close as they are right now?

Marie's hands lay lightly on his chest. Her eyes are closed, listening to their movements. He grasps her hips and begins to circle, gently grinding to penetrate deeper and deeper into her moist depths. She's still listening, waiting. He thrusts more powerfully, and she nods, in agreement. Her fingers press onto his chest's flesh. He pauses, watching her face. She frowns and her nails dig into his skin. Sam grips her hips and Marie begins to move her pelvis back and forth, faster and harder. She's back in control, wanting, needing to direct and own him. She falls on his chest and bites him in the neck, her body shuddering and shaking. Sam feels lust flood him from head to toe and can no longer hold back. Marie moans pushing herself deeper and deeper into his body, tilting her hips back and forth, back and forth. Sam peaks with an intensity that blasts his sense.

A knock at the door. "Sam? Are you asleep? What are you doing in there? We have to leave in a few minutes!" Chuck brays.

"Just a minute," Sam calls, another donkey-laugh answers. Sam looks into Marie's eyes. Her look is warm and full of love, but her body is as tense as a coiled snake, ready to strike.

"You have to go," she murmurs, kissing him and rising. She clamps the towel between her legs and elegantly as a dancer slips her dress over her naked body, eying him expectantly. Only a few seconds ago he had felt her moist, warm skin against his own. Now, she is fluttering away like a bird escaping a cat, reaching the safety of a high tree.

Sam would have preferred to stay in bed with Marie held tightly in his arms. He would have asked her what she expected from life after, whether she imagined him to be nothing but a diving adventurer, without any sense of responsibility. Foremost in his mind is the question he wants to ask her. Would she be his wife? He would forego just about anything to share his life with her. That the love between them clearly defines his priorities – to be with her. Then Chuck brought him back to reality, the spell was broken, the moment passed.

Marie blows him a kiss, smiling at him with eyes that speak of love. She turns gracefully, as she does all things, and leaves the room. "Chuck?" she calls down the hallway. The ghost of a thought flashes through Sam's mind but he rejects it immediately. Jealousy is the last thing he needs right now. He swings himself from the bed and stands on love-loose legs. It's time he got dressed.

FOUR

On their way to Zurich, Sam receives a call giving him the coordinates for the transfer location. He enters them into his GPS. The place turns out to be a former industrial area now used for commercial purposes, a Zurich neighborhood of the less savory sort. A second call comes in, this from a man with a heavy Swiss-German accent and far less gentlemanly manners. He tells Sam bluntly he will be the one to make the transfer and either he comes alone with the stones or he will shoot John before his eyes.

Sam shivers. A goose just walked over his grave. His breath is going quickly, sending small clouds that are rapidly squandered by the wind. A backpack is slung over his right shoulder, stuffed with one of the sweaters he had bought in Iceland. The stones are in another bag with Chuck, but Sam didn't want to show up empty-handed. It might be interpreted the wrong way. Sam does his best to relax. His evident nervousness is a dead give-away.

It's now quarter past eight in the evening. There are few street lanterns and the buildings are cloaked in darkness. Sam hears trains coming and going somewhere behind the buildings. Wet asphalt reflects the stingy light. A misty rain had set in about an hour ago and Sam can't help but think Nature plans this sort of thing. He does his best not to grin. There's not a soul to be seen and he assumes commuters avoid the area at night, taking a roundabout way to restaurants and homes.

He walks slowly and steadily to the only other car parked in the vicinity on a lot in front of a former assembly hall, now a concert venue. The dark limousine windows hide whoever is in there. On the other side of the street is an old factory, housing small business offices. No one's working late tonight.

His cellphone in his raincoat's inner pocket has a live connection to Chuck, who is waiting in the jeep in the entrance to a parking garage, kitty-corner to the limousine. Sam swallows and licks his dry lips before whispering, "Okay, they're here. I'm on my way." Something Chuck already knows as he is watching Sam through binoculars. He stops and long streams of mist escape from his mouth. He tries to gain control over his breath. His pulse thrums hard and fast against this throat. He feels like he did as a young boy, standing on the lip of the ten-meter diving board. Don't look down too long, his friends had advised him, or you'll lose your nerve. And don't think about the option of turning back or you'll never make the jump. The longer you wait, the harder it will be, just take a deep breath and jump! Back then, Sam outfoxed his terror by telling himself he was only pretending he was going to jump, he would stop before he actually jumped. He walked slowly to the end of the diving board and simply kept walking, laughing at his startled thoughts, wondering who had pushed him off the board.

Just keep walking, Sam says to himself, and his stress grin immediately spreads over his face. The tension in his stomach loosens and his breath streams deeply into his lungs. He's ready.

Chuck is ready, too, night vision binoculars pressed to his eyes. They had arrived early, and Sam parked out of sight. He walked behind the building complex in order to approach the meeting point from the opposite direction, making it appear as if he was coming from the train station. Alone. Chuck observes Sam's progress.

On the way to Zurich they had discussed their strategy, doing their best to consider all eventualities. They were well aware that they couldn't play out every possible scenario. You never know what's going on in another person's mind. Which goes for the two of us, too, Sam thought. There were just too many options. They would hand over John but not the money; they would notice the stones were missing; they would take the stones and kill Sam; John wouldn't be there...

And then, Sam isn't really sure about Chuck. Again, and again he pressed him to stick to the plan until Chuck gruffly spouted, "OKAY! You're the boss!" Still, Sam has his doubts.

During his military stint, Chuck was assigned to a crack unit. He was trained in hand-to-hand combat and when his unit was sent to protect an embassy, he had shot one of the terrorists. Chuck had told Sam the story one day as they were waiting on their snorkeling tourists. Sam was impressed, but not because he had killed a man. It was more Chuck's demeanor when telling. Business as usual, shot through Sam's mind at the time. From Chuck's point of view, he was just doing his job and saving people from a worse fate. He was neither proud of it nor did it seem to burden his conscience. It was just a story to pass the time. At least, that's how it came across to Sam. Still, it stuck with him and he often wonders just what kind of person Chuck really is. Why did he tell him that? How would Sam deal with a similar situation?

As a conscientious objector, Sam drove an ambulance during his mandatory civil service. The things he saw; dreadful accidents, squashed human flesh, severed limbs. Those and other images are only a casual trigger away. When they rise up in his mind again, his body reacts instinctively. His pulse begins to race, and his extremities stiffen, as if it were happening all over again. What on Earth would it be like to line a human being in the crosshairs, to feel the kickback when you pulled the trigger, to see the bullet you let loose tear away half of a man's head and to watch as he fell to ground like a sack of cement?

Maybe there are people who don't ask themselves such questions, who just accept the realities as they come. That doesn't make Chuck a killer. But Sam is still plagued by doubts. Can he rely on Chuck? Or is he's following his own agenda that he hasn't bothered to share with Sam or the others. Sam had made it perfectly clear that Chuck was not to act independently, he must stick to the plan and Sam will let him know what to do when. As far he knows, the mobile connection is still live, but Chuck did not respond. An answer would give them away.

About twenty meters from the limousine, Sam stops short. He raises his hands and signals to the backpack on his right. The headlights come on and Sam is momentarily blinded, the area suddenly bathed in light. Sam hears the car door opening, and man gets out of the car and stands behind the open door.

"Mr. Frei?" a thickly accented voice asks.

"Yes."

"Come closer please and place the stones on the hood of the car in such a way that your hands are visible at all times."

Sam approaches the car. He can't tell if the man is alone or if he's armed. Sam sets the backpack on the hood.

"Where's John?"

The passenger door opens, and a man steps out. Sam recognizes John from a photo Emma had shown him on her cellphone. Still, Sam asks, "John, are you all right?"

"John's fine," the man answers in John's stead. "So is his family and so is Jace."

"Where's Jace?" Sam insists. Apparently, Jace's mobile is off. They had tried to reach him several times while driving to Zurich.

"We kindly escorted Jace onto the train to Interlaken. His cellphone, however, is in John's pocket. So, you see, all your possessions are being returned to you. *Gut so*?"

NOT GOOD! Sam thought. Damn, they have no way to prove the man was telling the truth! Sam's breath quickened. Things are not under control.

"Okay, so where's the money?" Sam asks, his voice cracking under the strain.

"You give me the bag with the stones. We'll examine them. All's well, we'll transfer the money."

"That wasn't the arrangement," Sam replies, something steely possessing him. He suddenly feels like he's watching himself from a few feet away.

"You're right, but you must understand, we need assurance. John, you stay put," the man commands, moving around to the limousine's hood. Sam can see him better now and Chuck's moniker – he called him Gorilla – is more than precise. Dressed completely in black, Gorilla had the chest circumference of a wardrobe. His left hand, probably used to regularly crush heads, lifts and fingers open the backpack. His right hand remains in his trench-coat pocket. Sam stands still and serene as a stone. Gorilla gives a quick look into the backpack before reaching in and fishing for the stones. He then looks up to ensure that John is still standing behind the passenger door.

"That, *mein Freund*, is a mistake," he says softly.

"That wasn't the arrangement," he repeats Sam's sentence, somewhat surprised. Gorilla did have a name, although Sam and Chuck will never know what it is. Günter. And Günther thought it was going to be an easy job. Amateurs, Arik had told him when he gave him the contract. He thought he'd forego a partner this time and take the whole fifteen thousand for himself. Arik was an important customer, gave him regular work. Mostly security stuff, but some dirty jobs every now and then, when a deal didn't quite work out as Arik and his partners expected. Arik was a gentleman, so Günter was there when things became less genteel. Arik had actually suggested taking two snipers in case these dolts got the idea of diving deeper for more treasure. Especially this Sam, whom Günter recognizes from the photos Arik laid out before him, was a sly fox, not to be underestimated and he should keep a sharp eye on him. But Günter is a professional and plans his commissions himself. It's not the first time he's done such transfers and, until tonight, nothing had ever gone wrong. If he could forego the snipers, he could keep the entire commission for himself and pay off his gambling debts. Or could wager the whole sum and win it big. Lady Luck is on his side at the moment, he felt her caress last night, no doubt about it. His number came up in roulette twice in a row. Too bad he hadn't asked for an advance; he could have bet more than a lousy thou and his debts would now be history. He imagines getting the job done and returning to the tables tonight, taking advantage of his lucky streak. If all goes well, he'll be in the big money, walking out of the casino with a million in his pocket. Finally, rich! One of the big brass, and never have to get his hands dirty again. Easy money, Günter had thought on his way to the transfer.

If he had known just how much money was involved, how valuable the stones he was to collect, Günter might have had some greedy thoughts himself. But Arik was smart enough not to tell him, even though he knew Günter was incapable of deceiving him. Like all of Arik's employees, Günter is more than savvy to the syndicate's reach and power. Lead them not into temptation, is Arik's guiding principle, especially since Arik himself does not know exactly how valuable the diamonds will turn out to be. Naturally, they are worth more than the ten million he offered. He is a businessman and invests only where profit is a certainty. The true reason for his urgency is market stability. If word got out that any Tom, Dick and Harry could pick up diamonds scattered on the ground while taking their Sunday walk, the market would collapse, taking Arik and his associates down with it.

Günter had chosen the transfer location with care – dark, deserted and still practically in the middle of downtown Zurich. A place he knew like the back of his hand, having hung out there with his gang in his youth, bullying his classmates out of their pocket money. Easy money. All he had to do was flex his muscles a bit, metaphorically beating his chest, and people began to quake.

But this job is turning out to be less than easy. Günter feels his muscles tense and his pulse accelerate. His instincts are preparing for a fight. Damn! He senses there is going to trouble. Arik warned him that this was delicate job and that, in the event of difficulties, injured or dead were unacceptable. Günter was to be on his best behavior.

He now fervently wishes he had engaged the snipers as Arik had recommended.

He took a deep breath and swallowed.

"Where are the stones?" Günter asks quietly, almost kindly, while drawing his right hand from his coat pocket. The silver pistol gleams in the headlights and is aimed directly at John's head.

"Whoa, slow down, slow down," Sam gasps and talks toward his coat pocket, "Chuck, bring the stones."

Günter's eyes rise questioningly. Sam turns to the building on the other side of the street. Seconds later, Chuck is moving out of the driveway, carrying the backpack and approaching slowly.

"This is your last chance," Günter advises gently. "Come here and show me the stones."

Chuck reaches the car and methodically withdraws the stones, packed in plastic bags and sorted according to size, laying baggie for baggie on the hood as if arranging a display at a market. He pays no heed to John or Sam and avoids looking Gorilla in the eyes. Sam is reminded of Marek, the ranger's dog at Silfra. Chuck seems to be staring at the thug's chest when he turns to him.

Günter scans the booty and thinks a moment, "Okay, pack them back in the backpack and place it on the hood."

Sam can sense John's fear and tension, it matches his own. The air is electrified and both of them jump when two cats shriek, fighting over territory or a lady. Sam is shocked at the danger exuding from Günter and Chuck.

With excruciatingly slow indifference, Chuck begins to repack the stones, taking two steps around the hood toward the gunman.

"Stay where you are!" he growls, and Sam watches the gun swing toward Chuck. Chuck acts as if he hasn't heard and continues his slow-motion packing. A shot zings, chipping the pavement at Chuck's feet, ricocheting and howling off toward the concert hall.

Sam and John automatically crouch down in alarm but, unperturbed, Chuck merely looks down where the shot impacted. Then, just as calmly, he raises his head, follows the pistol's mouth and looks directly into his opponent's eyes.

The thin ray of a flashlight streams out from the building across from them. Günter glances up at the window where the light is coming from. A night watchman? He can't tell.

As if someone has flipped a switch, Chuck's left hand shoots out, grabs the revolver and presses it up and away. Almost too fast for Sam's eyes to follow, two stretched fingers of Chuck's right hand ram into Günter's throat. His left hand whips around, clasps the man's neck and yanks his head downward. Chuck's knee bounds with a crunching sound into the man's face. Günter falls to his knees. Chuck hammers the pistol hand on the car's hood until the weapon falls to the ground, useless. Snatching his ears and with a powerful jerk, Chuck twists his adversary's head sharply right. With a sickening snap, Günter alias Gorilla falls to the ground. Permanently. So much for his lucky streak.

In those few seconds, Sam forgets to breathe. He stands in front of the car paralyzed. He watches Chuck wrench open the limousine doors, flip open the trunk.

"Nothing! No money. Let's move!" Chuck calls to John and Sam. John's cowering on the ground, his head in his hands and Sam is rooted to the spot, staring at Chuck in dismay.

John moves to Sam and the two men stare down at the thug. "Fuck!" John whispers vehemently. A dark stain is spreading at the man's crotch. He's obviously dead. His neck broken. Sam remembers the sniper story Chuck told him and the uncomfortable feelings it had invoked. They were right.

"Come on," Chuck calls again softly, swinging both backpacks over his shoulder. No one moves. "We must get out of here. There's nothing you can do for him now."

He pulls on Sam's shoulder, pushing some button, and they all run to the jeep. Sam and John side by side with Chuck leading the way. Chuck automatically jumps into the driver's seat, Sam and John dive into the back. Sam has a fleeting déja vù as they pull out of the garage, round the building at a fast pace and take the road home.

FIVE

C huck opens the door to Sam's house and walks into the living room, not bothering to take off his boots. Sam and John follow, dazed.

Reclining on the sofa in a tight embrace are Emma and Jace. Piet and Marie occupy the overstuffed easy chairs. When Jace sees his cousin alive and well, he jumps up and packs him in a bear hug.

Emma rises slowly and looks at Sam and Chuck with glittering eyes. Daggers or gratitude? Sam can't tell.

Of course, they had called from the car. They learned that Jace had arrived. Arik and his people had escorted him to the train to Interlaken. Sam told Emma that they had John with them, alive and well, but there had been a hitch in the plan.

John draws Jace's cellphone from his pocket and returns it. He's a head taller than Jace and at least twice as broad. He's still puffing from the short walk up to the house. Jace nods his thanks and pulls John over to the sofa to sit next to Emma.

"What happened? You guys look rather battered, but all's well now and the nightmare's over," Emma remarks cheerfully.

John buries his head in his hands and a laden silence cloaks Emma's gaiety.

"Sure! All's well," Chuck replies huskily, unaccompanied by his usual grin and braying laugh.

Marie goes over to Sam, hugs him tightly and kisses him on the mouth. When her eyes meet his, she knows something went very wrong.

Sam untwines himself from her embrace but keeps hold of her arm. "Let's all sit down, and we'll tell you what happened."

"Shall I get the champagne? There are four bottles chilled and ready. Let's celebrate!" Piet cries enthusiastically, having missed all the signals to the contrary.

"Maybe later," Sam replies quietly.

Marie looks at Sam, then at Chuck and at John, who is still cradling his head in his hands.

"So, you didn't get the money." It is more a statement than a question.

"No, we didn't get the money. But we still have all the stones, and most importantly, Jace and John," Sam announces to the room in general.

"So, why do you all look like you've just come from funeral?" Emma asks.

"Because someone died," Chuck states calmly as he takes baggies from the backpack and lays them on the living room table.

Emma blanches and gasps, "Who? What on Earth went wrong?"

"The transfer didn't follow through as planned. The thug the syndicate sent didn't have any money with him. They wanted to examine the stones first and then would, allegedly, transfer the money. The gorilla was only there to collect the stones," Chuck reports blandly.

"And he died when he saw your ugly face? What did he have, a heart attack?" Piet's attempt to lighten the mood goes over like a lead balloon.

"Not quite. The guy suddenly pulled a gun on John while Chuck was unloading the diamonds," Sam interjects. The last thing he wants right now is to hear Chuck relate how he killed a man, making it sound like he's ordering goulash at a supermarket meat counter. On the drive back, the scene replayed over and over in his mind's eye while Chuck navigated the Swiss hills in silence and John sat next to him with his eyes closed, probably in shock. Would he have done the same? Of course, he didn't have Chuck's training, but would he have done his best to defend them? Shouldn't he and John be grateful? For all Sam knew, Gorilla could have had orders to kill one or both of them once he had the stones. They hadn't expected Sam to bring Chuck. That was their ace in the hole. Or did Chuck provoke the situation? Had he planned that from the get-go? When Chuck realized Gorilla was alone, did he simply kill the man in cold blood? Sam couldn't come to a clear conclusion, so he decided to see Chuck as their savior. Particularly in front of the others. They had enough on their plate as it is. Fighting among themselves would only complicate matters and that's the last thing they need. John and Jace are safe. But this is not over yet. Far from it.

"The situation was extremely precarious. The guy shot at our feet and Chuck reacted, overpowering him. I can't thank you enough, Chuck! You're amazing!" Sam says, demonstratively wrapping his arms around his 'hero.'

"And the man simply dropped dead?" Piet asks, the grin still on his face.

"With Chuck's help, yes. He had to make sure we were out of danger and in the struggle, he broke his neck." Sam was doing his best to sound casual, as if it had been an accident; a tragic chain reaction beyond anyone's control. Boys playing football; a hard tackle; rocks hidden beneath the sod; unprotected head crushed on undiscovered rock. Tragic.

Shocked silence.

Emma and Marie exchange glances. They look at Chuck, at Sam and finally at John. Emma's emotional register alters visibly from horrified pale to raging red, and shatters the silence, "ARE YOU OUT OF YOUR MINDS! We have Jace, John, a pile of stones and, by the way, A DEAD DIAMOND DELINQUENT! Why didn't you just give him the stones? Fuck the money! Do you know what this means?"

"Cool your jets, Missy. We wanted to give him the stones. We were just taking out the baggies. You ever stood in front of a loaded gun, Sweetcakes? Who says the guy wouldn't have simply shot us all once he had what he wanted, hm?" Chuck replies, his voice and face utterly unreadable.

"Chuck's right. We didn't go with the intention to kill anyone," Sam interjects before Emma could take a breath. "But who would have thought a few karate chops would snap a man's neck like dry twigs? I mean, seriously, he was the size of my refrigerator! But, naturally, we're in deep water, no doubt about it. We'll be hearing from these people until they get what they want, yet they were the ones who reneged on the arrangement. They should have sent the money as agreed."

"Wow!" Piet exclaimed hoarsely, "You broke his neck with your bare hands?" Evidently, he had done some preparatory celebrating. His eyes watery, his voice slack. Either Piet had no idea of the danger they were in or he simply didn't give a damn.

Jace has been following the conversation from the sofa, watching Sam and Chuck's volleyball bounce back and forth. He turns to his cousin, "Is that really what happened? So, why didn't you just give him the stones? The people in Zurich seemed quite reasonable. I wouldn't have thought they were looking for trouble."

"And how did you like having a pistol in your face?" Chuck interrupts. He has reached his limit on calm, cool and collected, coughs out a laugh and looks daggers at Jace.

"It was like Chuck described. I was terrified and still can't believe we got out of there alive," John tells him, his eyes locked on some unknown point of interest on the wall.

"Merde! What are we going to do?" Marie wonders.

"Well, I know what I'm going to do," Chuck declares, "I'm getting the hell out of here. I'll take one of the big stones and a few of the small ones. You guys can have the rest. Give them away if you want. Agreed?"

For a moment, Chuck's directness stunned them. He seems so sure.

Sam turns to John without responding to Chuck, "What exactly does your contact know about the stones?"

They all listened intently as John tells his side of the story.

"One of my dealers told me about a contact he had in the diamond syndicate, a group specializing in discreet diamond trade. He said it was not advisable to simply go to a jeweler and try to sell the stones. They're too rare. Thus, he got in touch with Arik and showed him the sample stones, talking about a few thousand carats. Neither my dealer nor Arik knows of the list you made in Tórshavn with the exact size and number of stones and their possible value. I didn't deem it prudent. Arik was enthusiastic. He wanted to know all about the stones, where they had come from, how many there were and if they all had the same purity. I explained that I didn't know myself and would be happy to introduce him to my client, if Arik was willing to negotiate a deal. Arik left it at that and promised to get in touch. He would need to talk to a few people but would contact me within two days. He was certain we could do business."

John was enjoying himself. The whole business was rife with just the sort of thrill that attracted him, a healthy mix of fear and suspense. As a teenager, the year preceding his A-levels, his classmates got wind of his ambition to become a goldsmith. He became the butt of endlessly cruel teasing. He was the chubby, reserved boy. The pants of his school uniform always sliding just that much too far down his rear end. In drawing class one day, as John was leaning bent over his work, one of the tanned jocks dropped a lit Chinese cracker into the crevice between his bottom and his pants. The explosion was no more than the slight bang of a pencil case hitting the floor, but John panicked as if chased by demons, fleeing the room with his hands down the back of his pants, groping for the small, hot cylinder. The teacher was at first puzzled but when he realized what was happening, he joined all the others in laughing until they cried.

John could hear their roars in the boy's room all the way down the hallway where he had his pants around his ankles and was spitting into his hands, trying to cool the blisters forming between his buttocks. From that day forward, he kept his head down and tried his best get through with some sense of pride intact. He failed. Mostly because the girls began to rub salt in his wounds with their snide and cutting remarks about the fat queer who thinks he can become an artist.

While apprenticed to a goldsmith, he realized he would never make a decent living with his artistry. It was meeting Nancy that lit a fire beneath his ambition. Something must be done. His 'spare tire,' as the boys in the locker room called his paunch would certainly repel such a pretty and intelligent girl. Not true, John thought to himself. He had seen the pretty wives of many a rotund jeweler at vocational school gatherings, including his boss's wife. Moon-faced and flabby, he had something the others didn't have. He was rich.

John then switched his major to Gemology. The science of stones. He learned how to assess the value of a stone and could tell you which mine it stemmed from, based on its structure and grain. He found he had a talent and was soon considered an expert. Particularly in the world of diamond traders, he was their dark horse.

His assessments were precise and accurate. His accountant's apparel, his reserved, respectful appearance and soft, high voice were desirable attributes. For the first time in life, he was taken seriously.

After graduating, he easily found a position with a large diamond trader, finding himself often drawn into shady business arrangements with people desiring to invest their black-market funds in diamonds or to make large sums invisible to the taxman. Powerful people willing to pay handsomely for discretion, trusting John and his boss, the company's owner.

Besides the money he brought in, earning him his dear Nancy and a comfortable life for them both, there were other pleasurable side-effects. John had become an important person, admired and respected. The discreet meetings with the rich and powerful gave him an inexplicable thrill, a high similar to indulging in the forbidden fruit of sexual adventures with someone other than his wife. But even more stimulating than lust. A secret he must keep, although the crime itself was negligible. He was addicted.

So, when his cousin Jace called and told him the bizarre story of how they had found the stones, he jumped at the chance to negotiate the deal. He had a sneaking suspicion that he was in over his head this time, but that was precisely what drew him like a moth to a flame. After the first meeting with Arik, he fretted no more. He expected it would be as it always is, plenty of discussion, doubts and haggling; negotiation tactics and, when all was said, they would agree on a price. And what a deal this will be! John had never been involved in a coup of such dimensions and he was sure Jace would pay him a handsome commission.

"But Arik turned up earlier. The next evening, while I was taking our cocker spaniel for a walk, this black limousine pulled up at the curb just as Becky was doing her business on a lamp post. The back door opened, and Arik leaned out, inviting me to get into the car. I refused. Arik got out of the car and suggested we walk a bit together. Without prelude, he told me it would be much better if I came with him. Surely, I didn't want my children to get hurt on their way to school or my wife while doing the daily shopping.

I couldn't believe my ears! Of course, it was often intimated that what when on behind closed doors is best forgotten as soon one left the room. That a long memory could be a dangerous thing. But never before had I been openly threatened. Truly terrifying was the gentle, cordial manner with which Arik threatened to harm my family. I was in shock and unable to move, merely stood there shaking like a leaf."

John remembered how his mind raced, searching manically for some kind of escape. He found none that would save not only him but Nancy and his children. His legs nearly failed him at the thought of something dreadful happening to his family. This man in his tailored anorak, his delicately accented words, his leather gloves and self-contained assurance. How he watched him, examining his terror as if he were some interesting specimen under a microscope! John felt his panic rising. At the mere snip of his fingers, Arik's people could erase his life. It was not fear for his own life that cracked his foundations, it was what his life constituted. To walk away unharmed only to lose the three people he loved most in this world flooded his being with a horror he could not even name. He felt his bladder loosen and knew he was about to wet his pants. He had heard that even the bravest soldier wet himself when a bullet penetrated the helmet of a comrade next to him, splattering brain matter as it exited. There are but three options open to him – fight, flight or play dead. John's instincts chose the third option. He stood there, incapable of moving as wet warmth trickled down his legs.

"Arik just stood there watching me, observing the impact of his words. I was in shock and I guess he knew that. At some point he placed his arm around me like a good friend and said things were not as dire as they seemed. I should just play along, and everything will work out fine. We will all live a long and happy life and it would all be well worth the trouble.

So, I brought Becky home, went to bathroom to wash up and change my clothes. When I came out, Nancy was already in her pajamas. She was dead tired and asked me sleepily where I had been all this time. I told her I had had a call and there was some urgent business I had to attend to. In school I had learned well how to bury my fear beneath my skin, so I think she believed me. I told her the commission would be generous and she could even start planning that holiday on the Maldives that she had been wishing for all these years. She shouldn't wait up; I could very well be gone all night. I took the lane leading behind our brown stone where the limo was waiting. They treated me well, even cordially you could say. But the whole time I was terrified something would go wrong. Arik had left no doubt that he was serious, deadly serious."

John concludes his narrative, taking a deep breath before jumping up hectically. "Oh my God! Nancy!" The last she had heard from him, he had had urgent business. That was yesterday evening. It was quite possible that she had already notified the police of his disappearance. John snatches Jace's cellphone from his hands and storms out of the room.

"Well," Piet remarks, "now we know that Arik and his buddies don't know how many and how good the stones are. That's good news."

"Yeah, true, but that's not the end of it. You can bet your life on that," Sam comments.

"What do you mean?" Marie asks nervously. "Do you think they'll make for our families or barge in here with a troop of thugs?"

Just as Sam draws breath to respond, his cellphone hums in his pocket. Anonymous call.

"Samuel Frei…" he answers and signaled the others to be quiet.

"Hello. If it's all right with you, I'd like to put on the loudspeaker. We're all here and will decide collectively," and he placed the mobile on the coffee table.

"Yes, Mr. Frei, we know where and with whom you are. Unfortunately, our arrangement did not follow through as planned. I apologize for our employee; his performance fell dreadfully short of our expectations. As you well know, this will not happen again. I hope you are all in good health?" Emma and Marie are appalled. The man speaks of his employee as if he were – was – a malfunctioning device.

"Can I assume I am speaking with Arik?" Sam asks.

"Yes, you may, but that is beside the point Mr. Frei," the nasal voice allows, continuing, "What interests me most is finding a solution that will spare you and your friends any further discomfort. If you will bear with me for a moment, I'd like to elucidate." As genteel as Arik's speech seems, his voice is cold, and his words carry an underlying threat. His use of the word discomfort felt like a gun at their heads.

Thus far, Sam only knew this man from the telephone. It was difficult to imagine what kind of person he really is. He reminds Sam of those godfathers in mafia films, calm, controlled, courteous and direct, leaving no doubt as to his intentions and what he is willing to do to attain his desires, an underlying threat beneath every polite word. John also knows very little about Arik. That he emigrated to the U.S.A. many years ago, is in his late fifties or early sixties, has thinning, salt and pepper hair and is obviously rich and powerful enough to control anything and anyone foolish enough to enter his realm. Or nearly. He certainly botched the transfer. Even Sam would have sent more than one man. He is tempted to call his bluff and tell him just as courteously to go to hell, but he thought of Arik's threats to John's family. Better to hear what he had to say.

"Shoot," Sam requests.

"Excellent. Now, excuse me when I seem to go rather far afield, but it is important that you all understand what is involved in disposing of your Iceland souvenirs. The stones do come from Iceland, am I right?"

"What does that have to with anything now!" Emma shouts, enraged. Sam shakes his head vehemently, hoping she gets the message and holds her tongue.

"I can well understand how distraught you are Emma, but please calm yourself," Arik says gently but firmly.

"As I was saying, the difficulty is the size and quality of your treasure. We are most happy for you but cannot allow such stones to enter the open market uncontrolled. This would result in a massive price collapse. We and our clients would lose a fortune and that is only the beginning. Once word got out on where the stones had been found, a gold rush – or better, a diamond rush –" here, Arik gives a gentle snort that they assume is laughter at his own little pun, "would ensue, whereby more stones could be found and diamonds would suddenly be worth no more than Swarovski stones. Do you follow? For decades, my colleagues and my humble self, have invested much in maintaining the high value of diamonds by ensuring they remain scarce. You may not approve of our methods, but that is a negligible irritation. Rest assured, though, that we and other related organizations will do our utmost to avert a price collapse. And our utmost is multifarious and highly inconsiderate. Do you catch my meaning? Please understand that I am eager to assist you, in both of our interests. But you can count yourselves lucky that only you and I are aware of your treasure."

Emma shudders, knowing that these people have already located all their families, where they shop, go to school, work…

"Certainly. We understand. What do you suggest?" Sam replies, looking each of them in the eye in turn. Marie and Emma roll their eyes in response, Piet nods, Chuck flips the bird, Jace shrugs and John, standing in the doorway, shakes his head.

"Fine, fine. Then we are agreed. My suggestion has not changed. You give us the stones in exchange for ten million U.S. dollars in cash and that is the end of it for you and your families. Over several years, me and my colleagues will gradually put the stones, cut into small lots, on the market. Wholly under our control. Naturally, we will make a profit, but that is only good and right, considering our time and effort."

"And what assurance do we have that the next delivery will not be a repeat performance of the last?"

"I, personally, will be meeting you. And Mr. Frei, are we all agreed that in this situation the police would be as of little assistance as further violence?"

"Sure…where and when?"

"We will meet tomorrow at nine across from the Backpacker Hotel at the Interlaken East train station. I will be in my car and expecting you. Agreed?"

"Yes."

"Oh, and Mr. Frei, I will be coming alone, but that does not mean I will be unprotected. I bring the money; you bring the stones – all of them. Should similar stones appear on the market we will immediately know from whence they came. If you all hold to the agreement, this will be our final meeting. You may begin new lives with the money, but I must insist you do so discreetly. Do we have your word?"

The group of friends exchange questioning glances. Sam takes a silent poll and receives a nod from each in turn.

"Our agreement is unanimous," Sam informs Arik.

"Delightful. Then until tomorrow. Enjoy your champagne...toot, toot, toot."

"How the hell does that creep know we have champagne on ice?" Piet yells while Sam takes his cellphone from the table and makes sure the connection is broken.

Chuck brays loudly, "Ha, ha! He's only bluffing!" No one else laughs. They look at each other and scan the room. Are they being observed this very minute? Are there mics implanted in the house? Big Brother is watching you! As if they all are having the same thought, a collective shudder courses through their bodies.

Excited talk erupts in the living room, but Sam withdraws into his mind, trying to get a grasp on how they could have possibly arrived at this juncture.

It was a miracle that they had survived Langjökull's eruption at all, out running the avalanche and reaching the antenna mast at the very last second, before the mud and ice devoured them. Then they found the diamonds and it seemed from one moment to the next they were stinking rich, even though no one knew how to turn them into cash. Come to think of it, the stones are like shares in a start-up, only theoretically valuable. As long as the clumps of carbon were still in their possession, nothing would change. They were still poor diving guides. Their attempt to sell the stones through John brought on that unspeakable situation that had cost a human life. They might have brought a fortune from Iceland, but they also brought the tsunami. They are hopelessly overwhelmed by the prospect of riches and all its implications – what to do with it, which risks are involved, which options they have. They are drowning in greed, desire, fear and lust, and all of them, including their families, have been put in terrible danger. For Christ's sake, what have they gotten themselves into?

Out on the terrace, Sam blows blue cigarillo smoke into the night sky. It's well past midnight. Lights on the far shore glitter and are mirrored in the lake's still, black water. All is quiet in the house. John went to bed almost immediately after the call from Arik. He'll be taking the first train to Zurich in the morning and try to catch a plane to Heathrow. Nancy panicked when he didn't come home, and the police were searching for him. He did his best to explain, only to have his wife and the police believe he had run off to Switzerland with his lover. They hoped the five small stones they had given to him would at least convince Nancy of his fealty.

Jace and Emma went to their room without another word. Sam feels for them. They had endangered a member of Jace's family, and the guilt lay heavy on their conscience.

They had talked to Barbu and he was doing fine. Thank God for small favors!

After tossing around the pros and cons, they decided they would give the syndicate only a portion of the stones tomorrow – mid-sized and small ones – in exchange for the ten million Arik promised. Giving them all the stones would be cutting their own collective throat! Just stupid. But what they will do with the rest of the stones? One thing is obvious; the stones will have to stay out of sight for a while. A long while.

Chuck puzzles Sam. Why is he suddenly satisfied with just one of the large stones? He doesn't even want his share of the cash! Is he simply taking a gamble? Of course, one large stone is worth much more than Chuck's cut of the ten million, but how does he intend to turn it into cash? Okay, Sam speculates, there's always the possibility he's making long-term plans and will wait ten years for the good life. But that just isn't Chuck, the I-want-it-all-and-I-want-it-now guy. So, what the hell is he playing at?

What a gigantic fustercluck, Sam broods when his thoughts are interrupted by the murmur of voices. He glances into the brightly lit living room. There's only Piet lounging on the sofa, feet on the table, sharing a romantic evening with a champagne bottle, holding it tenderly by the neck and smiling blissfully.

Sam moves over to the edge of the terrace and leans out and looks about the property. There, on the drive leading up to the house, he sees Chuck and Marie deep in conversation. Sam presses out his cigarillo and puts the stub in his pants pocket. What the hell?

Marie's left hand is on Chuck's shoulder and with the other she gently strokes his face. Sam feels a blow to his gut, knocking his breath away.

"…things are going well…" he hears Chuck say softly. "…Sam and the others are playing along."

"I'm so glad you made it back safely," Marie whispers. Or at least that's what Sam believes he hears.

Their tête-à-tête is abruptly interrupted when Chuck slips away from Marie and looks up in Sam's direction. He must have seen his shadow drawn on the water, backlit by the terrace lights. Sam withdraws smoothly as a cat, returns to the terrace center and lights up another cigarillo. Moments later, he hears soft footfalls approaching from behind.

"A penny for your thoughts, chérie," Marie says to his back and slips her arms around him, pressing her body close.

"Hmmm… much has happened over the last few hours," he murmurs, hoping Marie doesn't notice his heart hammering in his chest. He doesn't know what to think. What does Chuck mean, playing along? How? At what? Is he getting paranoid? Sam turns and kisses Marie on the mouth, her lips warm and pliant. She snuggles up to him. Is her intimacy with Chuck just an expression of friendship?

Marie slips from his arms, takes his hand and leads him into the house.

Sam gently removes himself. "You go ahead, darling, I'll be right with you," he says with a warm smile.

"Don't be too long, chérie, or I'll fall asleep," she replies mischievously and gracefully steps into the house.

The moment Marie is out of sight, Sam's smile drops off his face. He replays the scene, his manager's instincts stirring. What did you call it when someone tried to convince you an X was a U? Isn't that what he feels like now? On the one hand clear as day, on the other so smooth. As smooth as Marie's skin. But he's not in a boardroom now, is he? No one's trying to dupe him, Marie would never do such a thing! He knows her too well. Doesn't he? His track record with relationships was not exactly brilliant. He had been taken in time and again. When the whole thing blew up in his face, friends and colleagues would ask him with all his business acumen, why hadn't he seen what was obvious to everyone else? The lady was playing him for a fool. His naïve faith and yearning for the woman of his dreams was far easier to bamboozle than his unfailing manager instincts.

Okay. Again. It was evident that Chuck and Marie had once been intimate, judging by the closeness he had witnessed below. Marie was concerned about Chuck, had stroked his cheek. But she hadn't kissed or hugged him. She was like that with everyone she cared for, loving and physical.

So far so good. No reason for jealousy. But why did they have to go off alone to talk? And what did Chuck mean by "playing along?" How? Did he and Marie have some kind of arrangement regarding the large stone?

Try as he may, Sam cannot find a satisfying explanation. Still, the facts gave him nothing with which he could confront the two of them. If they had something to hide from him, his questions would only trigger their anger, or, in Chuck's case, his sarcastic laughter. Marie would probably be offended that he didn't trust her. In any case, probing the issue would only cause friction, if not an outright conflict. He would never learn the truth. He'll just have to wait, watch and listen, to make dead certain there's something to confront before risking humiliation. Yes, that's the best plan, Sam thinks and turns to go into the house.

Chicken shit! His manager mind complains. You're just afraid to rock the boat and risk losing Marie. Sam goes to the bar to drown the voice in cognac before he joins Marie under the blankets.

SIX

Sipping carefully on his scalding hot coffee, Sam reclines in one of the wicker chairs on the terrace. It's not quite six am. He slept poorly, while Marie slept the sleep of the innocent beside him. Dozing, waking, staring at the ceiling, he finally slipped out of bed at dawn. Naked, he climbed down the narrow ladder from the terrace into the lake. The icy water, less than ten degrees Celsius, snatched him up like a giant's fist, squeezing the air from his lungs. Holding tightly to the ladder, he took a few more steps down until he was submerged up to his neck. After a while, his solar plexus relaxed a few millimeters and he could draw short, careful breaths. These few moments of exclusive physicality abruptly ended the carousel his thoughts were trapped on, the ponies galloping off into the distance. As Sam felt his equilibrium return, he pulled himself up onto the terrace in one smooth motion.

Sea gulls circle the lake, calling raucously. The mist slowly rises from the water, climbing the mountain slopes across from his house. At this hour, the milky-white tatters hover level with Sam's terrace. He feels the gentle wind at his back and the sun's warmth lifting the air from the water.

Soon, the mist will vanish completely, and vison will be unobstructed.

"You're up early," Piet grumbles, leaning on the French doors, clearly hungover. "And you're packed and ready to go," he adds nodding to the backpack at Sam's feet.

Piet turns inside and comes back with a steaming cup of coffee. "How much did you pack for the vultures?" he asks, falling heavily into a wicker chair.

"As we agreed. About half of the mid-sized and all the smaller stones."

"That leaves one big one for us and one for Chuck."

Sam nods, keeping his eyes on the mountains.

"He's an odd guy, Chuck. That's why the ladies never stick with him long. Marie didn't."

Sam turns and look Piet directly in the eyes.

"Oops! You didn't know? Shit…Well, now you do."

"I knew there was something between them. They were a couple?"

"Yeah. Damn. Me and my big mouth," Piet mumbles ashamedly and hides his face in the coffee steam.

"Too late."

"Okay, okay, I can understand you're surprised, but that was at least three months ago. As soon as Marie joined the team, Chuck set his sights on her and didn't let up until he had her. He's a terrier, you know that. He wined and dined her, was as charming as a prince. But it didn't last long…"

Sam makes no comment, waiting for Piet to continue.

"Anyway," Piet continues, "one evening Marie was sitting in the kitchen crying her eyes out. I made her a cup of tea and sat her down on the sofa. She then told me how screwed up Chuck is; that he was cold and heartless and forbade her to look at him when they were in bed together. You can imagine, what a turn-off that must be. Chuck wanted a slave, not a partner. Maybe that's what he found in Seydür."

Sam takes all this in silently, the questions still in his eyes as he looks at Piet.

"That's it, Sam. That's all I know. But, hey, Marie seems to be really happy with you."

"How can you tell?" Sam asks curiously. Piet just shakes his head, smiling. Either he can't or won't tell Sam more. For a short moment, Sam thinks about telling him what he observed last night, but immediately decides against it. Piet will only think he's jealous and playing along merely refers to their decision what to give Arik. But how is that playing along? It was ultimately Emma's suggestion, not Chuck's. Sam has an uneasy feeling that Chuck meant something altogether different.

"What are you going to do with your share of the money?" Piet shatters his brooding. "In just a few hours we are all going to be rather well-to-do." Sam shrugs and grins. Sure, he's thought about it, but hasn't come up with a clear aim or project he would like to launch or something worth investing time and money. He supposes he'll just have to wait and see what inspires him.

Piet laughs and heaves himself from the chair. He points at Sam's coffee cup, but Sam's had enough.

Piet shuffles back inside, shaking his head. Incomprehensible, he thinks. He knows exactly what he's going to do. First, he will buy his mother a small apartment on the canals in Leiden, his Dutch hometown. Nothing fancy, just a nice place in a nice neighborhood where people could afford to be kind, instead of battling for every scrap falling from the table of those better off like in the tenements where he spent his childhood. Maybe she could even find a job again, have a normal life. What she would have had if he hadn't come along. She often told him she once dreamed of studying and becoming a university professor. Eventually, he had realized that she could have had anything if it wasn't for him; could have gone to school if she hadn't had to look after him. That was one of the reasons he had wanted to move out as soon as possible. It wasn't only the constantly rotating freeloaders she brought home. No, he wanted her to be free. Free of him, free of the responsibility a child entailed; free to go back to school. But things hadn't worked out like that. Even after he was gone, her life continued along the same strain and he was a failure, unable to finance his own psychology studies, even though he worked every night and weekend at the supermarket. It just wasn't enough. Eventually, after repeatedly falling asleep at lectures, they threw him out. Then the job in logistics. That really sucked. And although he loves working as a diving instructor, the pay is pathetic. He has a real talent for motivating his students, helping them confront their fears. He knows exactly how to give people the space they need to overcome uncertainty and move on, most of them earning their diving license. He is proud of that.

Now, that he has the cash, maybe he will resume his studies, earn his diploma and open a practice in Rotterdam. Maybe even start a family of his own, what a thought! One he'd never had before. But then again, he could open up his own diving base, he really loved diving. Whatever, he'd be rich enough to do whatever made him happy.

He could care less about the remaining stones. But…come to think of it, they could bring in another wave of cash! Maybe he's thinking too small – the meager dreams of a poverty-stricken child. If John calculated correctly, they were worth ten times as much as the ones they're selling this morning. But they have to hide them for a while. Still, he could help others like himself; give them a chance to get out of the ghetto, to study. He could make a change in people's lives and on the planet. He'd be a hero! He'd go down in history! Piet, the savior of Leiden! Yes, he should think big, enough could be more than enough to change the world. He'll see to that.

"Take care!" Chuck grins, waving both hands at them all. John, too, is saying his goodbyes. They had already taken leave of Sam, who left a quarter of an hour ago to meet Arik. Jace will accompany them to the West train station. Their train to the airport leaves at nine thirty and they hope to catch a plane back to London. Emma and Marie can't believe Chuck is leaving before Sam gets back.

"Don't you want to wait and see how things went with Sam?" Marie asks, surprised at his sudden rush to leave.

"I've got my booty as agreed and it's time to get out of Disneyland. It's much too tidy here, I need to get back to my stomping grounds. Let's hope John and I get a flight back to merry old England," Chuck barks a laugh, slapping John on the shoulder. John for his part seems rather uncomfortable with his traveling companion and looks to Jace.

"If that's the way you want to play it," Jace eyes Chuck skeptically. "Wouldn't you rather have your share of the money?"

"I'm a gambler! If I can sell the stone, I'll have more than twenty times your pitiful ten million. I owe you one!"

"Sure, if you can sell it," John murmurs.

"Yeah, IF. And if things go wrong, you'll only set the next pack of wolves on our tail," Emma protests. "Not a very attractive idea!"

"Sweetheart trust me! I would never tell anyone about you all," Chuck brays at her.

"Yeah, sure, trust you! Now there's a joke," Marie teases. "Come on, big guy, give me a hug." And she presses him close.

"Sam will certainly be back soon," Piet remarks, breaking up the sustained embrace.

"I'm not big on long goodbyes, let's go," Chuck finalizes, putting his arm around John's shoulders and practically pushing him to the door. He rolls his eyes at Jace to indicate they should make tracks now and waits impatiently while the never-ending round of hugs and well wishes starts up again. Jeez.

A million and a half each! Peanuts! They're all wound up like kids on their birthday and can't wait to open their presents. Not for him. Arik and the syndicate can stick their ten million where the sun doesn't shine. He'll find someone willing to pay what his stone is worth. For a moment there, he was tempted to take the whole backpack and disappear. Without his help, they wouldn't have anything. Who got them out of Þingvellir Park in one piece? Who took care of Gorilla before he could rip them off? But, what the hell, there are still the rest of the stones and he can sniff out their hiding place. No hurry.

What a pack of pussies. They wouldn't have lasted a day at training. Wouldn't have even passed muster, that's for certain. Once, when he dropped to one knee in exhaustion, vomiting up his breakfast, his sergeant lashed into him, "Who do you think you are? Get the fuck up and move! What a loser, you limp-dicked pussy! Too much for you, huh?" They intentionally recruited social underdogs for their elite troops. Poor kids who hadn't yet succumbed to the bottle or needle, surviving on the streets of Manchester's slums. The ones who didn't back down when push came to shove but stood defiantly, daring their foe to make that fatal move. C'mon, boy, try me. The ones determined to claw over the swamp walls, no matter who was stepping on their fingers, trying to push them back. He wanted more than survival, he wanted to live. On that day, he got up, spit the puke from his mouth and swore he would make it or die trying. He turned to steel, unyielding and knew what he wanted. He only went to Iceland because the pay was good, and he could save enough money to open his own security firm. But everything's changed now. He has his elbows on the wall and is about to pull himself up and over.

Why settle for a beggar's breakfast when he can have the whole buffet? First, he'll find Seydür, the only woman who has ever understood him. She thinks like he does, doesn't pussyfoot around. He has to find her, then his life can finally begin! He's rich and wants it all, nothing less will do. Finally, Jace and John join him at the door. Chuck turns and gives Marie a wink and then they're gone.

Things got very quiet once the three men were out the door. Emma, Marie and Piet sit down on the sofa like crows on the wire and wait for Sam. There is an uncomfortable silence. Something's troubling them, but what is it? Chuck takes off with one of the large stones, foregoing his share of the cash. Even John seems to have little interest in the four hundred thousand they offered. That was the sum left over after dividing ten million by six. After all, it was John who made the contact with Arik, and he had certainly earned it. He seemed happy with the offer, but Piet thought he read disappointment in his face. Had he expected a full cut? Wasn't it enough compensation for all he had gone through? Still, he had bid farewell heartily enough, pressing his spongy wet cheek to each cheek, kissing the air three times. Maybe Piet was seeing things. John himself said he couldn't very well take so much cash on the plane. What would he say if customs found it?

And that led to the next issue. How are they going to transfer the money to their respective banks without raising suspicion? Well, Sam intimated he could solve that one. How?

Then there is Chuck's odd behavior. The man especially unsettles Piet. Emma seems glad to be rid of him and no one really knows what Jace thinks. Marie is apparently the only one of them that can make sense of Chuck.

The moments of waiting stretch into hours.

SEVEN

Sam strolls from East Station toward the boulevard. He spots the limousine parked on the left side of the street. An opaque window behind the driver's seat slides down and Sam approaches the car. A thin man, bordering on reedy, in a black Kashmir coat gets out, swipes a strain of silvery hair from his face and smiles at Sam. Small, brown eyes twinkle above an oversized eagle's beak dominating his face.

Sam is surprised. For some reason he imagined Arik to be tall and hefty, his movements deliberate. A Hollywood gangster boss. This man is nearly a head shorter than he is, his body language speaking awkwardly, like a teenager not yet quite at home in his skin. Alert eyes look out from Arik's facial façade of casual sovereignty. Sam can almost hear the clockwork in his brain whirring; a blitz chess player analyzing multiple moves and variations as well as his opponent's reactions and options, all within seconds. And yet, Arik manages to exude the serenity of a Buddhist monk. He is certainly at home with his power. Sam imagines his family hasn't the slightest idea of his shady business and friends take him for an adept dealer in antique books and artworks. The perfect cover for Arik's brutal boss-man doings in representing a powerful diamond syndicate. Diamonds are a girl's best friend. Perhaps. But they are also one of the major sources of diabolical greed and inhuman suffering, funding illegal weapons for countless warlords in Africa and the Mideast.

Small, gangly and seemingly harmless, this man is a keen strategist devoid of sentiment. In a word, he's dangerous. Sam takes all this in as Arik steps from his limousine.

"Mr. Frei! I am Arik. It's a pleasure to finally make your acquaintance. Please, do take a seat."

Sam removes the backpack from his shoulder and gets in the car without a word. The driver's seat is vacant, so he assumes the meat packer standing a few meters ahead on the sidewalk with a button in his ear is Arik's driver and bodyguard. Sam is relieved. No driver, no hasty retreat with Sam in the back seat. Suddenly, he realizes the risk he's taking meeting these people alone. He's certain that aside from the thug posing on the curb for his benefit, there is sure to be a sniper or two eying the birthmark on Sam's forehead through crosshairs. If something should go wrong, the last thing Sam would hear is small popping sound, like drawing a rubber cork from a bottle. His body would fall to the ground and Arik would wave his bodyguard over to lift Sam into the car. With a cloth pressed to his head, bystanders would think he had taken ill and his friends were bringing him to the hospital. Pity. But the mountain trails are calling, and we really must take a selfie in front of that stunning alpine landscape! The scene and Sam would be forgotten in a trice. His body never found. But it's too late now.

Arik takes his place next to Sam and begins, finger for finger, to remove his kid gloves. He offers Sam his bare hand, but Sam only looks at him in silence.

"Come, come Mr. Frei. If anyone has a right to be offended it is I. I am the one who lost an employee, and it was no easy task cleaning the area without drawing undesired attention."

"Fine, Mr.?" Sam replies, pressing the narrow hand.

"Oh, all of my friends simply call me Arik. And a business partner is always a friend, Sam. May I call you Sam?"

"Do you have the money with you this time…Arik?" Sam concedes with a smile.

"Delightful! Already we're friends. But to answer your question, naturally. It is in a travel case in the trunk."

Arik slides a bit to the side and pushes a button. The armrest between them sinks into the seat and a travel case comes into view. Apparently, the limousine is used often for such transactions. Maybe there's another button to catapult Sam into the trunk alongside the suitcase? And just because there's a container, doesn't mean it's full of money. What if there's nothing but a sweater in there? A potshot at Sam's ploy at the first transfer attempt?

Arik resumes his seat next to Sam and ogles the backpack at his feet. He eyes Sam expectantly, rubbing his hands with a child's anticipation. When Sam only looks at him silently, Arik catches the unspoken question.

"My goodness, Sam! Do you really suspect there's no money in the case? I would think there would be a modicum of trust between friends, wouldn't there?"

Even if there was money in the case, that doesn't mean Arik would just let him walk away with it. Damn! He should have taken some precautions of his own; thought of a way to ensure his own safety. He should have placed half of the stones in a safety deposit box at the bank, only giving Arik the key when he was sure he had the money. As it is, he'll just have to play it Arik's way.

Sam lifts the bag up and places it between them.

"With your permission, Sam?" Without waiting for his reply, Arik opens the zipper and pulls out one of the baggies with mid-sized stones. He takes a small magnifying glass from his coat pocket and fits it onto his left eye.

"Oh Lord!" he exclaims softly, whistling through his teeth.

Sam watches the little man as he holds various stones against the interior light, gazing at them intently with his mouth half-open. Like an art lover viewing an original Picasso for the first time, he cocks his head and squints his eyes. Is this for real? Arik gently lifts a stone as if it were a precious work of art, utterly overwhelmed. No, strike the art lover. This man is a pious believer, a worshipper, holding a shred of Jesus' shroud in his hands.

But what does he worship? Sam asks himself. Nature's beauty in a stone she created by millions of years of unimaginable pressure and heat? Or are his prayers directed toward the god setting the stone's current market price? Arik tears himself from his contemplation and looks at Sam with glowing eyes.

"Do you know how extraordinary these stones are, how breathtakingly clear and pure? It's a shame we will have to cut most of them down into small pieces! Or perhaps I should simply keep them as they are, taking them out of the safe on special occasions to feast on their beauty. What say you, Sam?"

Sam is rather discomfited. It seems that Arik has no interest in how many stones there are.

"There are other largish ones, but not so large, and the small ones, too," Sam replies without answering what he believes to be a rhetorical question. One by one, he takes the baggies out of the backpack and sets them between himself and Arik. Arik gazes at him through his unhindered right eye and snatches up another baggie with mid-sized stones like a magpie. Same procedure. Arik whistles and examines the stones. Without warning, the magnifying glass vanishes, and Arik is gazing intently at Sam, as if he, too, were a rare stone.

Arik, Sam now realizes, is akin to a junkie-dealer who has just scored a kilo of the purest stuff and can hardly wait for his first fix. He knows that when he exercises restraint, he will have an exquisite supply until the end of his days, cutting and selling the rest for an exorbitant price. This combination of gentle worship, fanatical greed and hopeless addiction confuses Sam. He realizes his imagination had been simple and one dimensional. He had imagined Arik would just assess the stones' quality and value before making the deal. A business transaction, nothing more. Yet, here is a man walking the fine line between madness, obsession and the exacting control of an adept racketeer.

Sam senses there is more than money involved. There is a higher force behind supreme wealth and its name is Power. The Power to play God, shaping the world according to his own ideas and ideologies. The Power to overrule any resistance or opposition quickly and easily. Not with violence, this meeting made clear that Arik prefers weapons such as influence, cleverness, deliberation and money; to manipulate the sheep for his own ends or lull them into submissiveness so he can steer the world in his desired direction. Power, the force behind human cruelty and betrayal since the beginning of time. An insatiable, never-ending hunger is what Sam sees in Arik's eyes; the ecstasy of Power channeled through wealth.

Arik places the stone back in the baggie, stacking them all neatly on top of one another. He sighs, "What a tragedy that the source of these stones now lies beneath tons of lava. Or a blessing. Should there be more of this caliber, I would soon be an impoverished man," Arik pronounces and giggles almost girlishly, rapping his thigh gently. He shows little interest in the other stones, holding up each baggie for a short moment before putting them back in the backpack.

"How did you come to these stones, Sam? And how did you transport them to Switzerland?" Arik asks conversationally. "My friend John told us you were running from a lahar."

"We escaped the lahar over a side road rising from the valley floor. We found the diamonds in a fissure. I never would have given them a second glance, but a colleague spotted them right away. We stuffed them into the side pockets of our diving suits. Why do you ask?"

Arik give Sam a critical glance, "There were six of you, right?"

"Yes, Sam replies, wondering what Arik is getting at and how he knows these details. Probably from John, he's Jace's cousin, not just an assessor, so Jace must have told him the whole story.

Arik stacks the baggies, six to a pile and looks at them. He lifts each pile and tests their weight. So that's it, Sam thinks. He doesn't believe we gave him all the stones.

Arik looks long into Sam's eyes, searching for the smallest sign of uncertainty. Sam nods.

Acting the innocent would only spur Arik's suspicions.

"Six pockets. I threw the half of mine away. They were heavy and rasped on my leg every step I took. We walked twenty kilometers over crevices and lava fields. It was a hard trek and we didn't really know if we were carrying diamonds or just rocks. A pocket is about the size of those baggies. Those are ALL the stones, you got it?"

"I looked into the matter and some of these suits have two pockets, one on each side..." Arik replies smoothly.

"That's right, but only the Fifth Element models. Two of us were wearing Fifth Element suits. The others only had one pocket," Sam answers just as smoothly, raising his eyebrows and raising his palms. He is getting tired of this game, even if Arik is on the right track. On the way to meet Arik he had repeated a thousand times that he had all the stones, convincing his short-term memory that it really was true. He shakes his head and shoots daggers at Arik. Enough. He opens his mouth to speak but Arik assures him with a nod and raised thumbs that it's okay. It seems Sam has convinced him, too.

"So, dear Sam, and now to business. However, there is one small change of plans…"

Sam stiffens. What now? Is this another con? Heat rises from Sam's belly and he would like nothing more than to smash his fist into this puny creep's face, grab the backpack with the stones and get the hell out of there. His hands clench into fists.

"How do you know that I'm unarmed? I could easily cut your throat, you know. Of course, your thugs would have a field day with me, but you'd be as dead as a doornail," Sam hisses in Arik's face.

Arik gapes at Sam in horror for a split second before his mouth begins to tremble.

"Oh, come now, Sam," Arik laughs. "You should see your face! Not to worry. It is only that the money is in Swiss francs and not U.S. dollars. Otherwise, I would have needed a truck to transport it." Arik finds the situation highly amusing, laughing long and heartily, eventually drawing a silk hank from his inner pocket and delicately dabbing at his eyes.

"Ten million Swiss francs. Ten thousand new thousand-franc notes. Stacked, they make a pile one meter high, have a volume of just fourteen liters, weighing fifteen kilos. Easily fitting into a small, rolling suitcase. I do hope you forgive me for not bringing U.S. dollars. In hundred-dollar notes, ten million would have filled a trolley. The Swiss francs will even give you a small profit when exchanged. But we don't want to be ungenerous," Arik assured him with a wink.

He loves Switzerland, Arik rhapsodizes. Not only for its wonderful approach to money. Swiss chocolate is also wonderful. Sam fears he will dissolve into laughter again, but Arik sobers quickly. His business depends on large cash transactions that leave no trail of bank transfers and suchlike. There is no other country in the world where you can carry around such large sums of native currency as is required for the discreet diamond trade. Does Sam have any idea how voluminous one hundred thousand one hundred-dollar notes are? Another rhetorical question.

"You could have brought it in five hundred-euro notes, I could have carried that easily," Sam remarks drily.

"Why Sam, you're rather greedy. The exchange rate as it is, I would not have been able to round off the sum," Arik justifies smugly, lowering the backrest behind them. He pulls the case out and opens the latches. Now it's Sam's turn to view the booty. He takes several neatly bound stacks of hundred thousand-franc notes and views them at random against the interior light. Watermark and silver thread are visible. He pulls another stack from the bottom and examines this as well. It looks like Arik has kept his word.

"Successful transactions must be sealed with a toast," Arik remarks, opening a small bar built into the paneling. Before Sam could protest, he finds a half-full tumble of vodka in his hand.

"A custom retained from my younger years in Moscow. Nostrovia!"

They chink glasses and Sam takes a tiny sip while Arik easily drinks down the whole glass. He eyes Sam's glass and gently removes it. "Forgive me Sam, but I am in somewhat of a hurry. Who knows? Perhaps we will meet again, should you ever attend another volcanic eruption," Arik says, his eyes on the case between them. Sam nods, taking the case and opening the car door. He bends down, "Be well, Arik. Take good care of yourself."

"Yes, yes, Mr. Frei," Arik replies absently. "You, too." Apparently, they are no longer such good friends.

Sam rolls the case along the boulevard, heading for his jeep. He hears the smacking click of a door closing. A sound unique to expensive cars. A moment later, the limousine purrs softly to life and pulls away. As they take the curve, the wheels squeal although they are going no faster than a crawl. Must be armored.

Arik is gone and Sam allows himself to begin to believe they have done it. He looks around discreetly for anyone lurking, ready to wrest the case from his hand. Unless the mother with her baby strolling along the boulevard has a pistol in her purse, he can discover no threat. The case's wheels glide almost silently over the pavement. This is no cheap trolley. Its body is made of brushed aluminum and is as aerodynamic as an airplane's rump. Sam remembers eying these symbols of success enviously, especially those well-used, slightly banged-up specimens, plastered with decals from nearly every country in the world. Those were his parvenu days as he was finally sent off into the world, aiming to conquer it. Back then, he thought owning such a traveling case would show them all he had made it; would be the ultimate sign of success and wealth. He had traveled the entire world and made it his own. It had taken him nearly twenty years to wield this status symbol, only to discover he was fed up with traveling. By the time he turned his back on his old life, his case displayed but a meager collection of dents and international airport decals. He'd had enough.

The smooth sound of rubber wheels on asphalt reawakened the elation he felt as he proudly marched to the departure gate, his new case in tow. Today, he is strolling along, pulling a carefree future; the summer air, delectable; the birds singing sweetly just for him. He feels young again, full of energy!

How can that be? How is it possible that fifteen kilos of printed paper in a travel case makes him feel young and hopeful again? What kind of power is that?

EIGHT

Six stacks of thousand-franc notes, each amounting to one point six million are lined up on the coffee table in the living room.

When Sam came home, he was grinning from ear to ear. They gathered on the terrace around the case. Sam opened it. Gawking at so much money, and it belongs to them! Sam neatly divided up the money and placed the stacks on the table.

Jace and Emma each snatch up a pile, fanning out the crisp new Swiss notes in their fingers like playing cards. Hard to believe they were real.

Piet must be having the same thoughts and asks how they could be sure the notes are not forged. Sam suggests cashing one in at the bank tomorrow. Then they would know for sure.

Emma, practical as ever, throws out the question of how they would get the money to their respective homes. They certainly couldn't simply transfer it onto their accounts without raising questions and suspicions. And carrying it onto a plane would be even riskier. After tossing the issue back and forth, they decided to shrink-wrap the bundles and take it home by land. Piet, Jace and Emma would take trains home, confident they would not be controlled at the borders. No one with a European passport is these days.

Emma had called Barbu with the good news and he had promised to get back to them as soon as he could arrange to come to Switzerland. Upon ending the call, her face was wet with tears. So much has happened, they have been through hell and back; have lost friends like Simi and Ian and now they are rich, drinking a brew of happy providence bitterly seasoned with pain and grief. It is a plunging and climbing rollercoaster ride of emotions and Sam eventually fetches the last bottle of champagne from the cellar to sooth their turbulent hearts.

The entire evening, Marie is unusually quiet. Now, as they lay side by side in bed, Sam remembers eavesdropping on her conversation with Chuck and his stomach begins churning. Not yet, he tells himself, wait a while, watch a while. He'll broach the subject later.

"You've been so quiet. Everything okay?" Sam asks gently.

In reply, Marie nestles her head on his shoulder and plays with this chest hair. "It's just all so confusing and frightens me, too."

"What frightens you?" Sam whispers.

"I'm just not so sure being rich is really the boon it's made out to be. Crazy isn't it? Somehow, I just can't believe it's true, that this is the end of it, that Arik and his people would just give us the money and we all live happily ever after."

"Yeah, I've thought about that, too. We need to carefully consider what to do with the other stones and how to hide our money. We need to be prepared."

"Yes, and that's exactly what I mean. Money! What a headache!" Marie remarks, tittering softly.

"Oh yeah, but the joys it brings will eventually show themselves. We will never have to worry about money again. For me, that's the height of happiness. Until five years ago, I had nothing but money worries, as long as I can remember," Sam chortles, stroking her hair.

"Same here. But it's a double-edged sword. As far back as I can remember, the worst fights between my parents were always about money," Marie murmurs, after a pause.

And for the first time, she begins to share this part of her life with Sam. She recalls the teasing in kindergarten when she came wearing her brother's hand-me-downs. She tells him how later in school the other children asked if she had a papa since she never talked about him. And then, still later, how her poverty made her feel so unspeakably ex- cluded because she never had the right clothes, the right stuff, the right whatever it took to belong to the in crowd. She tells him about her deep- seated teenage rage against her mother for not providing her with a father; for denying her the riding lessons all other girls had; for not giving her the guitar she begged for year after year as a birthday gift. Finally, at seventeen, she ran off with her boyfriend, dropping out of school although she was a good student and had made it to the upper classes. She tells Sam about the months of squatting in abandoned houses, of drugs and al- cohol until one day, in a back alley where they would hang out, a street social worker approached her, asking if she might like to come by the youth center. Despite her gang's scornful laughter, she went along anyway and that was where she met René, one of the social workers there. René had a diving school. He took her on, letting her work in exchange for lessons. She earned her diving li- cense and spent the next years working and learning to become a diving instructor. Finally, at twenty-five, she had done it. She was an officially recognized diving instructor and had the diploma to prove it.

"I'm sorry your childhood was so hard, but you've come a long way since then," Sam tries to comfort her, caressing her trembling shoulder.

Marie lies on his shoulder, her hot tears falling onto his arm. What can he say? He simply holds her close, his thoughts wandering from her story to his own. He wonders what impact the sudden wealth will have on his life.

He has discarded his former dream of opening his own diving shop. Thinking it over now, it merely seems exhausting. Sure, he wants to dive. But for his own pleasure. Why would he invest his money only to spend twelve hours a day, seven days a week doing donkey work for tourists? Not to mention all the hassle with taxes, advertising, scheduling – Lord, no. Who needs it? Not with a million tax-free Swiss francs to play with! Still, it's not enough money to really make a dent in the world's needy and marginalized, so what should he do? Sit back and enjoy the ride? Isn't he a bit too young to retire?

Taking an honest look at the past decade, it was never money he missed. He had earned well. But even before that, money had never been a major issue. The truth is that he had always felt the lack of a true partner. He longed to, and still longs to, belong to someone. He longs for intimacy and human warmth, for someone with whom he could share his life and passions.

Could this someone be Marie? Is their age difference really that big of a deal? What are her plans? He hasn't a clue.

Sam turns and stretches out beside her. Side by side, face to face, he studies her red-rimmed eyes. Taking a deep breath, he is ready to tell her what he had overheard and how it has troubled him since then; ready to ask her what is between her and Chuck. Maybe he has the courage because she trusted him first? She opened herself to him, shared her experiences. She trusted him, so it's his turn to trust her. But before he can say anything, she lays a finger on his lips, pulls him closer and covers his lips with gentle kisses. She kisses his eyes and holds his head in her hands. "Come to me, chérie," she whispers in his ear. Sam raises his head and looks at her. She looks back, her eyes liquid and warm without the hunger they usually show when they are in bed together. This is something he hasn't seen before, something soft and vulnerable, seeking and offering shelter, seeking and offering surrender. Her eyes speak of souls united, saying, "I am yours."

Marie pulls her nightie up around her neck and Sam helps her slip it over head. He squirms out of his clothes. Marie lays still and waits for him. She is open, unconditionally, waiting for him to shine on her. His chest brushes lightly over her breasts and Marie moans softly. There, where their bodies touch, sparks fly. Marie pulls Sam close, closer, opening her legs and wrapping them tenderly around his back. She follows every movement on his face, her mouth open like a fascinated child watching a butterfly emerge from its cocoon. She watches the wrinkles around his eyes undulate and his closed lids tremble. He is so serious, concentrated and firm. Never had she thought a much older man could arouse her so deeply. His well-trained body feels so wonderfully solid. His muscles are more yielding, less knotty, than those of younger men she has held. Sam is warm, his skin soft. He opens himself to her, reveals himself as he is, shows her that he shares her need for love and acceptance. It is her closeness as well as her body that stirs him.

Marie feels his erection on her belly, and she is melting with desire. She wants him inside her, to fill her need until all she can perceive is him. Slowly, and then again more slowly, she draws him into her with her legs around his hips. Millimeter for millimeter, flooding her body, heart and senses with his intensity. Sam gasps and moans, burying his face in her hair. Filled, she lies very still as a powerful wave rolls in, washing warmly and profoundly through her body, from the bottom of her feet to the ends of her hair. Her legs quiver, she pants and bites Sam in his shoulder to vent the fireworks coursing through her. Replete, her legs slide gently down onto the bed.

Riding the wave, Sam begins to move slowly and rhythmically. Tender, yet demanding. Marie is amazed as her body and soul rise to meet him. She wants to surrender. Utterly. She had always needed control in order to feel pleasure and savors all the more this moment of complete release, this new, astounding trust. She knows Sam will hold her, catch her, no matter how far and long she falls.

Wordlessly, they lie next to each other holding hands, like teenagers honoring their first slow dance, a rite of passage. Mute, blissful, their hearts beating forcefully as one, they begin to sway gently to the tune of an unheard love song. Marie gives herself in Sam's care, he leads her, turns and presses her to him, never letting go of her hand. They listen to their breath, panting, moaning, stare into each other's eyes. The music increases in tempo and volume, they follow its course, rising higher and higher to the peak of their rapture. Never before has she climaxed so fully.

Together they sail over the ocean of their passion until the tides settle and wash them gently onto a warm beach where they lay entwined in profound union. The cool air dries their sweat-bathed bodies, their fingers tenderly interlaced.

Sam is enthralled. Never before has he had such profound sex, merging far more than their bodies. He doesn't believe in something like a soul, but this was more than sexual satisfaction. He remembered the first time he made love to a young woman. The same sensation of happiness and amazement filled him now.

How was it for Marie? He turns his head slightly to ask her and saw she had fallen asleep, her breathing deep and regular. He enjoys this secret moment, the freedom to gaze at her as long as he likes while she slept. He takes in the symmetry of her facial features, her clear skin, her relaxed mouth, so serious and calm, her beautiful, tangled hair that frames her face like ivy. Do I love this woman? What else could this be in his heart? What else hurts so good but love?

NINE

Minute by minute, mountain slopes cast their shadows further and further over the lake. As the sun sinks below the peak, so does the temperature on the water. Sam's small motorboat is mirrored in the glassy surface.

Marie gets up and turns for Sam to close the zipper on her brand new, cherry red, dry diving suit. Her stunning shape is accentuated by the second skin. Sam would much rather peel her out than zip her up as he lays his hand on her hips to carefully turn her to an angle better suited to the current purpose. The boat rocks slightly.

Yesterday, they all drove to Bern to buy new suits, paying in cash. Prior to their shopping spree, Sam had changed a couple thousand-franc notes at his bank. He is Swiss, he lives there and the people at his bank know him. Not that that would help him if Arik had given him forged bills, triggering the little red light on the bank's scanner. But all was well, the notes were authentic. For a moment, Sam just stood there addled, his hand full of Swiss hundred-franc notes. "Would you like an envelope?" the lady at the counter asked, smiling at his wonder.

They then went to the diving shop and bought two dry suits and a sturdy, nylon mesh bag as well as renting out a buoyancy device for Marie and two bottles of compressed air. Afterwards, in the car, Piet had laughed and asked why they even bothered to rent equipment when they could have bought the store's entire inventory. Now there's a sensible thought, Emma commented drily. Just how fast and conspicuously does he want to get rid of his money? At that rate, he'll be broke within the year.

Now, Emma is standing in the boat's tiny engine room, slowly guiding the vessel toward a sheer wall rising well a hundred meters from the black water. It is a good choice. The wall plunges perpendicular another two hundred eighty meters to the bottom of Lake Brienz. Sam knows the place from earlier diving excursions. He also knows that at about thirty meters' depth there is a small ledge before the wall vanishes in the deeps. A perfect cache for the remaining diamonds.

It took them three days of discussion to decide on the right place to hide the stones for several years. They agreed it was essential to hide the stones somewhere safe from the syndicate. Agreed, it must be somewhere none of them could reach alone, removing all temptation. Tempers heated and cooled several times throughout the discussion until Sam came up with the ledge far below the water. It was ideal. It would take at least three of them to retrieve the bags from their chosen hidey-hole and nothing welded them together more than diving.

Shrink-wrapped in plastic baggies, the stones lay in the mesh bag on the boat floor. The plan is to anchor the bag with trigger hooks to a steel cable threaded through several pitons screwed into the granite. The material would hold for years, much longer than they would probably need, since there is very little current so far below the surface.

Piet and Jace help Marie and Sam into the rest of their equipment. Before cutting the motor, Emma maneuvers the boat into position a mere meter or two from the wall. Sam and Marie sit side by side on the railing, give the O.K. sign and fall backwards into the water.

Beneath the water's surface, Sam removes his hands from his mask and diving regulator and stretches his body. Breathing deeply between his teeth, he fills his lungs with regulator air, making a hissing sound. Swaddled in underwater silence, Sam feels tranquility wash over and through him.

Floating, he gazes at the blackness beneath him. How he had missed this amazing grace! To be utterly at one with oneself, his thoughts wholly in the here and now, his body and spirit weightless. While still on the boat, he would have been sorely tried to recognize or describe it. Now, blanketed in water, it is there, crystal clear.

He looks back at Marie and senses she is experiencing a similar ecstasy. She is on her back, barely a meter below the surface with her regulator in her hand, idly blowing bubbles and watching them rise. Sam taps her on the shoulder, and she puts the regulator back in her mouth. Her eyes shining in the murky light, they rise up and break the surface.

Jace and Piet are grinning broadly when the Sam and Marie reappear and pump up their buoyancy vests. This is something they all share, their love of diving. They hand their water-bound friends lamp, trigger hooks and mesh bag, which Sam snaps onto his vest. He turns on the lamp and gives first Piet and Jace, then Marie, the okay signal. Marie replies with her thumb pointing down – let's dive!

Shoulder on shoulder they paddle toward the wall. A few seconds later, massive rock appears in the cone of light, stretching off to the left and right. Otherworldly beauty. Ancient grey-black granite structures, escapees from the last ice age's glacier as over millennia it carved out the valley and the lake's basin. Sam shines the lamp upwards, pinpointing the boat's location. He can't remember exactly, but the ledge is somewhere in the center of the three-hundred-meter broad cliff wall. Moving east and downwards, they should hit upon the place soon. He checks his compass, air supply and diving calculator. Eight meters below the surface and nothing but darkness surrounds them. The lamp shines like a deep-sea creature.

Although they are neither touching nor audibly communicating, Sam feels a deep, permeating bond with Marie. His breath resonates in his ears, and he holds the next one to perceive her airy bubbles. He glances back and sees her warm brown eyes behind her mask. Despite the cold that quietly creeps through his suit, despite the black abyss beneath him, he feels uniquely snug and secure.

With a hand signal, Marie asks if everything's okay with Sam. She shrugs her shoulders and grins behind her mouthpiece. Like pantomimes, divers learn to communication their thoughts and feelings by employing the eloquence of body language. Sam reads her loud and clear! How do you feel? I'm doing fine! Diving again! What a wonderful, strange feeling! Sam nods, gives the O.K. sign and floats over to stroke her arm. He removes his mouthpiece and forms a kiss with his lips. Marie wags her finger, her eyes laughing. Sam signals his concession and turns his thumbs down. They have a job to do.

Slowly, a solemn act of surrender, they sink in the motionless water. Occasionally, air hisses into their dry suits, offsetting the increasing water pressure and controlling their free fall.

Twenty-five meters' depth. Palm flat, Sam moves his hand back and forth, indicating they will remain at this depth. He then points eastward along the wall and glides ahead, flippers paddling calmly, Marie alongside between him and the stone wall, the mesh bag on its hook trailing behind.

A few moments later, the ledge appears. Disturbed by the lamplight, a pair of bass erect their thorny dorsal fins and vanish below in a cloud of silt. Marie and Sam float down and kneel face to face on the ledge. Sam checks his instruments. Depth: thirty-two meters; air: seventy-five percent remaining; diving time so far: twelve minutes. Marie does the same and gives the go-ahead. They still have more than a hundred and fifty psi in their compressed air tank. Sam grins, remembering how often, at thirty meters' depth, over-excited diving students had used up their air reserves, beating a retreat to the surface after a mere two minutes. They still have around ten minutes to anchor the mesh bag and ascend without making decompression stops.

Sam hands Marie one of the folding grappling hooks to anchor the bag. He finds a crack in the wall and a second one next to the first, twists the hook end into the crack and triggers the device. The hooks are strong enough to catch a climber when he or she falls. Here, they will only have a few hundred grams to hold. He threads the steel cable through the hooks and passes it to Marie, who does the same and passes the cable back to him. An uninformed observer watching from a distance would be puzzled by the mysteriously illuminated fingers dancing in the dark.

Sam then attaches the mesh bag to the cable with trigger hooks, adding a loose stone for good measure. Done, Marie signaled okay and waved her hands to come closer to Sam, sliding over the ledge on her knees. The lamps attached to each left wrist, bathed their faces in diffuse light. Marie removed her mouthpiece and pressed a kiss onto Sam's mask. Although her head was tightly encased in the neoprene diving hood; although, beneath her mask, only her pale grey, icy lips – so similar to the lips of a corpse – were exposed, she seemed to him sensual and warm. Sam tries to enclose her in a hug, but she wags her finger again and points at their diving computer. They've been underwater for twenty-two minutes, it's time to surface. They paddle away from the wall and ledge, ascending slowly, their eyes glued to the calculator's numbers. At five meters' depth, they stop rising and breath steadily to decompress the nitrogen in their blood stream.

Cloaked in nothingness, they hold each other close, like astronauts let loose in space. No air, no light, no gravity. Time is a foreign element, only remarked by their calculators, stoically ticking off the seconds until three minutes have passed and they can break the surface. The thrumming of a motor reaches their ears. Emma, attentive as ever, has noticed their bubbles on the surface and is coming to retrieve them.

Sam rubs Marie's shoulders to accelerate her blood circulation. He, too, is still feeling the cold. Practically shrink-wrapped in their new dry suits, they had remained completely dry. All the same, they had spent nearly fifteen minutes at thirty meters' depth in Lake Brienz and at four degrees Celsius – according to their diving calculator's display – they had quickly lost body heat. Jace has prepared hot chocolate laced with rum and Sam gratefully wraps his icy hands around the mug. Emma guides the boat in a long curve to the landing dock below Sam's house.

"Now, a hot shower," Marie announces and jumps from the boat. Without waiting for the others, she scampers up the path in her thermal one-piece, eager for warmth.

Emma moors the boat and the four of them carry the rented equipment to the jeep in front of the house. In a matter of minutes, they are comfortably seated around the open fireplace in the living room.

That went well. All in all, except for the unfortunate first meeting with Arik's gorilla, they are satisfied with themselves. The stones are cached, the money distributed and tucked away. Each of them has an additional five stones in a tiny draw-string bag. Emergency reserves. Since giving Barbu such a bag, and Chuck had taken his, it had become a tacit agreement that all of them should have one. Not only for the funds it might provide. Like an amulet or sign of their solidarity, each of them carried the leather bag around their necks. A tangible memory of all they have survived together, of their unity.

They've done all they can. All that's left is to wait for Barbu, give him his share and fill him in on developments. And then?

Piet is anxious to get back to Holland. He is not sure whether he wants to go back to college or try and set up his own diving base in Iceland. Jace and Emma remind him that it will still be a few years before Iceland has rebuilt its city and infrastructure. Then another year or two before they venture into tourism again. He would be better off going back to college.

For their part, Emma and Jace want to get home to their families. A few days ago, they had announced their intention to marry. Piet offered his condolences while Marie joyfully hugged Emma. Sam was touched. Apparently, the idea of marriage is more than amenable to Marie, judging from how thrilled she is at the prospect of their friends' nuptials. But when she asked Emma and Jace if they plan on having children, his sandcastle crumbled. Marie would hardly want an aging granddaddy for her children. He'll never know until he asks, though, and plans to keep his eyes and heart open for a suitable moment.

TEN

"Be right with you," Sam calls from the little garden beside the house. Emma wants to get going. She offered to take the train and collect Barbu at the long-distance bus station in Zurich.

Early that morning, Piet and Jace had taken the jeep to Bern to return the leased equipment. It was already three days overdue. Once there, though, they called with a change of plan. They wanted to re-rent the equipment and go on a diving tour of Lake Neuchâtel. Emma pulled a face when she heard she wouldn't have the jeep but gave the go-ahead anyway. To be honest, she hated right-side driving. In Iceland she was more than happy to leave the driving to someone else. She agreed to meet Barbu and bring him back on the train. They all missed diving, so why shouldn't the two have good time?

Listening in on the call, Marie couldn't help feeling slighted. How could they do that without her? Piet promised they would go again tomorrow. Maybe they could all go together? He just laughed when Emma mentioned the need for more equipment. Let that be my concern, he replied. He was the logistics whiz, remember?

Marie cut the call with a smile on her face. It wouldn't surprise her if they came home with half of the shop's inventory. She nearly called them back and asked them to bring that fantastic Apeks cold-water diving regulator she had admired in the store where they had bought their suits. She had never been able to afford Apeks equipment. A British firm, they developed their products with professional divers from around the world. Doubtlessly, the best on the market when it comes to durable, reliable gear. But quality has its price, of course, and now she could pay. After Sam cashed in a few thousands at the bank without a hitch, they had each taken a couple thousand-Swiss-franc notes from their stash and followed suit. Naturally, they didn't all go at once, but waited a day or two before the next one went to the bank. Nevertheless, suspicion had been aroused and when it was Marie's turn, the teller asked to see her passport and called in to validate her identity. Afterward, when the notes were cleared, the lady apologized to Marie for the inconvenience. There had been an unusual number of thousand-franc notes turning up over the last days and she had been instructed to verify identity the next time. Everything's fine, she said and paid out the requested change with a smile.

They would have to be more cautious and not draw attention to themselves.

Grunting with effort, Sam slid the life-sized, meditating Buddha carved of granite back into position. In a small hollow beneath the statue, Sam had just stashed the remaining large raw diamond. He didn't know why he hadn't left it with the other stones beneath the water. It was a gut feeling. Has wealth already infected him with suspicion? Is this a betrayal of his friends' trust? He hopes not. For whatever reason, though, the stone is now hidden in his garden. It just feels right.

He slaps his hands clean on his pants and sashays through the garden to the terrace. Marie and Emma are waiting impatiently at the door. Sam checks his watch. The train doesn't leave for another fifteen minutes. Plenty of time to walk down to the station together.

Emma squints in the sun as she waits on the curb at the vast long-distance bus station. Temperatures have risen noticeably. After weeks of heavy fog obscuring the sun, the sky is clear once more. The ash has finally dispersed or found a resting place on cars, buses, streets, houses and all kinds of foliage. Instead of yellow, springtime pollen dust, vehicles were coated in grey and efforts to clean it off resulted in slippery, grey-brown slime. Lines at the carwash were long and Saturdays were dedicated to cleaning new layers of dust from windows

Katla and the volcano group at Langjökull have settled down, although Katla is still spewing steam and occasionally coughing up a bit of ash. Prognoses, however, expect things to return to normal. Whether you can believe what the TV reporters tell you, is another thing altogether. Most airlines are on the dole, limping along until the powers that be give the all-clear. Nearly all air-lanes have been reopened, but passengers should be prepared for last-minute cancellations due to ash clouds on the radar screens blocking the route. For most travelers, this isn't worth the hassle and ticket sales have hit an all-time low since the eruptions. More unsettling and omnipresent is the shortage of fresh foods. Agriculture was hit hard, and tons of toxic vegetables and fruits had to be destroyed, making fresh foods more expensive than ever. Eggs, milk, cheese and meats have vanished from the supermarkets. The ash in grass, hay, grains and other feed rendered them unfit for human consumption. Emma's mum wrote that milk is impossible to get in England and the elderlies are reminded of the times of scarcity following World War II. There's not enough of anything, she reported, topped by an economic crisis. Who knows where it will end? But, for the most part, people are pulling together. What can be shared is shared and help is quickly found.

While waiting for the bus from Munich, Emma wonders how the people in Iceland are holding up. She knows the international monetary fund and EU ministers have provided generous credit. Hourly, freighters and ferries are transporting construction material and machines, medical aid, temporary shelter, as well as everything else necessary for survival. Aerial photographs on TV news programs make it look like a moving bridge or conveyor belt rolling endlessly from England to Iceland. Survival is in Icelanders' blood. For centuries, epidemics and natural disasters have literally been the cost of living on Iceland. They'll make it, it's in their DNA.

The bus is running late. Barbu had called with his travel plans. It was a veritable odyssey, but he was used to it. Since flying is too unreliable and insanely expensive, to boot, he said he'll take the bus from Bucharest to Munich and catch the next bus from Munich to Zurich. He's been on the road for a couple of days now.

And here it comes! Turning into the station parking lot, the huge vehicle stops with a sigh of brakes. The doors hiss open and passengers pour out and crowd around the luggage compartment. Where's Barbu?

Emma spots him with his backpack over his shoulder and walking toward the station, his head moving back and forth, scanning the area.

"Barbuuu!" Emma shouts. Hearing his name, he stops and turns. His eyes light up when he discovers Emma and they both start running at the same time, colliding on the wide stretch of asphalt, they take each other in a tight hug.

"So good to see you!" Barbu exclaims, his eyes wet. Emma playfully punches him in the side. She feels the same. Locking arms, she points to the bus station. "I'm afraid you'll have to take one more train."

"Who cares?" he smiles, "with such a wonderful traveling companion?"

Settled in their compartment, Emma gives Barbu a good once-over. He had always been reserved but very kind. Now, his silence carried an air of sorrow, his smile masking worry.

"Tell me how you're doing," Emma says softly, placing her hand on his knee. Barbu shakes his head and tears begin to pour down his cheeks.

"Simi?"

"Sure, but that's not all. His death was so senseless, and my parents are devastated. My father can't take it in and runs around like a robot."

"I'm so, so sorry," Emma says tearfully, switching to his bench so she can take him in her arms.

"But that's not all, Emma. When did you last talk to your parents?"

"Three days ago, why?"

"Because I talked to my parents this morning and they have had visitors. Men in dark suits drove up in a limousine. They were asking for me. My mother nearly died of fright. When she was a young girl, her father was taken away by *Securitate*, the Romanian secret service. She never saw him again."

"Are you telling me, the secret service is after you?"

"No, of course not. The *Securitate* doesn't exist anymore. The men said they had been sent by the syndicate and extended greetings from Arik."

Emma's jaw dropped.

"It took me nearly an hour on the phone to convince them it had nothing to do with government and that I hadn't done anything wrong. I told them I knew the men from Iceland and they only wanted to know if there was anything we needed. I'm pretty sure they didn't believe me. The big, black car, their suits and how they spoke – these people are not the solicitous sort."

Emma stares at Barbu unseeingly, her mouth still open, until he gives her a nudge.

Her face comes to life and she shrieks at him, "What are you saying?" She roots in her coat pocket for her cellphone, Barbu watching her uneasily as she swipes the display and chooses a number. She looks at him with enormous eyes and places a finger over her lips.

"They're not answering," she says. Just as Barbu opens his mouth to say something, Emma's cellphone vibrates. She looks at the display, incoming call, Mum & Dad. She takes the call, her eyes now slits, fixed on Barbu's eyes, her breath rapid.

"Hi Mum! Yes, I'm fine. Sure, I'm sure, why do you ask?"

"Who was there?" Emma asks. "And what did they want? They were asking after me? But…calm down Mum…calm down. Tell me from the beginning, okay?"

Barbu observes Emma repeatedly comb her hair with her fingers, rub her face and neck. She obviously wants to say something but gets no further than drawing breath to speak. He can hear the static buzz of her mother's uninterruptible narrative.

"Mom…really, everything's fine. I understand, you're worried. Of course, I'll call you back as soon as I've talked to them and cleared things up. Yes, yes, not to worry, I'm really okay. I'll be in touch. I love you, too, Mum and give Dad a kiss from me."

Emma tapped the display and ended the call. For a moment, she simply stared at the phone. She then told Barbu that her parents had also received a visit this morning from the same people – limo, suits, subtly threatening – who were asking after her. They also asked, overly casually, if Emma's brother would be home from college next weekend, but his fraternity brothers couldn't say exactly. Finally, her mother gave her greetings from someone called Arik who claimed to be a friend of the family and just wanted to know if everyone was doing well. The men assured her – which only served to frighten her more – dear Emma was safe in Switzerland with her diving

friends. Unfortunately, the friends had an out-
standing debt with Arik's organization and, try as
they may, they cannot reach any of them. And he,
Arik's emissary, merely wanted to make sure that
all is well, and no one finds themselves in unneces-
sary danger. Bastards! Her mum was beside herself and after they left, her dad called the police
and then M16, demanding to know what the
devil's going on and what Emma could have possibly done to merit such treatment. Of course, they
hadn't a clue about it. Bastards, bastards, bastards!

"Are Piet and Jace back?" Emma storms into
the living room, Barbu hot on her heels. Sam and
Marie, lounging back to back on the sofa, look up
from their books in surprise.

"Barbu!" Marie calls happily, jumping up and
clasping him tightly in her arms.

"What's up?" Sam asks a disheveled Emma,
getting up to greet Barbu, if Marie would give him
a chance. She doesn't look like she will any time
soon, though.

"You were right," Emma replies caustically. "It's
not over yet, the shit's going to hit the fan any

moment now." She hurls her coat and bag vehemently on a chair.

Sam wants to question her further, but at that moment his cellphone hums on the coffee table. Emma's eyes narrow and she nods toward his cellphone. Anonymous caller on the display. Sam picks up the phone and takes the call, "Samuel Frei?"

"Ah, Mr. Frei, how fortunate I could reach you so quickly. I hear the Emma and Barbu have arrived and my sources inform me that Jace and Piet are packing up at the lake."

"You're well up to date, Arik. What do you want?" Sam responds calmly, looking sternly at the others while placing his finger on his lips. He turns on the speaker.

"Quite the manager, Mr. Frei, that simplifies matters. With your permission, I'll come straight to the point. As you may have surmised, the money we supplied for the stones was not our own but came from our three largest clients. They are quite enthusiastic!"

"I'm happy for you. So that's why you're shadowing us?" Sam asks, his voice overly polite while Emma slowly slides her hand over her throat and flips the cellphone the bird.

"In a sense, yes, Mr. Frei." Sam doesn't give Arik the satisfaction of responding. He waits in silence.

"Then allow me to explain. Our clients are concerned that more such unusually exquisite stones could appear on the market, sending the price plummeting. If you recall, we spoke of just this peril when we met in my car?"

"Certainly."

"That's good to hear, Sam. Then you will also recall we offered to see to the matter, discreetly and civilized. We are your friends in this matter, Sam, you should know that," Arik continues. No longer Mr. Frei? Sam's face wrinkles in disgust.

"Ah, so, friends?" he asks tersely.

"Without a doubt Sam. As proof, I can assure you we did not tell our clients about your nocturnal diving tour. We can assume you weren't fishing for sweet-water crabs by the cliff. But let that not concern us now."

"What do you want, Arik?" Sam asks again, careful not to allow the fear that has settled heavily in his stomach reach his voice. Looking up, he sees Marie and Emma are going through similar turmoil.

"It's quite simple. You accompany us to Iceland and bring us to the place where you found the stones. Nothing more," Arik explains lightly, quite chattily in fact. "Oh yes, I nearly forgot, my people are watching over you and your families for your own protection. Our foremost concern is that we all come through this precarious situation in one piece. But we must bring it to an expedited close. I have things well under control for the moment, but patience has its limits. I sincerely regret pressing you, but the issue is urgent. Could you be prepared to depart tomorrow? Our jet will be waiting at Bern airport and a driver will collect you tomorrow morning. Shall we say, at seven?"

"Can I consult my friends and get back to you?" Sam questions them with his eyes.

"Unfortunately, no, Sam. I need your assent now," Arik cuts him off.

"Fine, Mr. Arik, agreed. But I'm warning you! If you do not stop frightening my family this minute, God help you!" Emma screams, ignoring Sam's wild gesturing.

"There appears to be a disruption in the line, some kind of static, I couldn't quite catch what you said, Sam," Arik remarks drily.

"I hear you clearly, Arik. Yes, we seem to have no choice in the matter. But once we've shown you the place and have returned safe and sound to Switzerland, it's over. Truly over. Do I have your word?" Sam asks, showing Emma a stiff, flat hand. Stop!

"You have my word Sam – and you do too, Emma," Arik replies, his voice gravely serious for the first time.

"Then until tomorrow at seven," Sam says and cuts the call without waiting for a response.

ELEVEN

"I just don't trust them. There seems to be no end to it," Emma says, shaking her curls as she sits cross-legged across from Jace on the bed, taking comfort from the woolly, over-sized sweater encasing her.

It was nearly eight before Piet and Jace returned from their diving tour. They were totally pumped, had had a fantastic day with three rounds of diving and a shopping tour for accessories they needed to perfect their gear. Piet had bought a set of Apeks diving regulators for Marie, complete with gift-wrapping. If it hadn't been for their predicament, she probably would have been ecstatic. But as things were, she barely managed a smile and a whispered thank you.

That the syndicate is hounding them is one thing, but that they have now involved their families is more than they can bear. Jace and Piet immediately called their mothers as soon they were filled in on the situation, but no one had turned up there. Not yet.

"Hmmm..." Jace mumbles, clacking his beer to hers and stroking his beard. Emma musses his damp, matted hair. She understands how tired he is, he had had an exciting, exhausting day. Particularly draining is the cold that creeps into your bones and makes itself at home there. Swiss lakes warm up to twenty degree in summer but when you dive down to twenty meters' depth, the temperatures remain a chilly four to eight degrees Celsius. In Iceland, in the Silfra Crack, the water never warmed over two degrees Celsius. When you spend the entire day just a tad less than warm, a hot shower was sedative enough, you could even skip the beer.

"Doesn't seem to bother you much. No wonder, your people have been left in peace so far," Emma tries to awaken his interest again.

Jace sits up. Looks his love in the eyes and strokes her flushed cheeks, offering what comfort he could, "You're frightened, I understand that perfectly well…but we have no other choice than to wait. They have to leave us alone when they know where we found the diamonds. What else could they possibly want?"

"What makes you think they will leave us alone?" Emma asks, aggrieved.

"John explained it to me. Diamond prices, like every other commodity, are set according to supply and demand. The prices have risen steadily over the years because the global supply has always been slightly less than the demand. What were once emerging nations are now globally important industrial nations and diamonds are an excellent status symbol. At the same time, recent laws are making it more and more difficult for the obscenely wealthy to avoid taxes or to invest their dirty money. Storing a million dollars' worth of diamonds in a safety deposit box at the bank is an attractive alternative. Diamond investments can't be traced, they're discreet, portable and quite lucrative. A stone bought in 2000 for fifteen thousand dollars is now worth twenty-eight thousand."

"I still don't understand what that has to do with us!" Emma remarks, confused.

John continues, "Yeah, it's strange. These are golden days for Arik and his people. Our discovery could cause an instant rise in diamond supply, something the syndicate and anyone investing illicit earnings fear. That's their boogeyman, their demon. The syndicate must control the market, come hell or high water, and that means knowing and controlling the source. I'm sure they plan on exploiting the find site, although I haven't a clue as to how they want to do it. But when they have that under control, there's nothing more they can possibly want from us, don't you see? Even though they apparently know that we didn't give them all the stones we have. Or maybe Arik was bluffing. Whatever. Those few stones we do have just aren't worth the trouble, I'm sure of that." John tries to make this sound like a conviction instead of the wishful thinking it really is.

"Exactly! They won't need us anymore. So, what's to stop them from making sure we don't tell anyone else? You catch my meaning?"

Jace nods. He hadn't thought of that, but Emma was right.

"In any case, I spoke with John today and everything seems okay on his end. Nancy knows the truth now and has finally stopped jumping at shadows. So far, no one has shown up at their place." Emma takes a large gulp of beer.

"You talked to John? I've been trying to reach him for days, but he never picked up the phone. Interesting. Maybe he's still really pissed off and doesn't want to talk to me."

"He's not ticked off, he's just had a terrible fright. He probably has nightmares about Arik's monstrous hooknose," Emma makes a weak stab at lightening the mood, paving the way for what she has to tell him.

"How do you know Arik has a honker? Have you ever seen him?" Jace asks.

"Of course not, sweetie. I don't know, I just imagine him with one. Or maybe Sam mentioned it?"

"Not that I can recall…but, tell me Emma, did the guy get in touch with you? Do you know him? You have to tell me," Jace insists. Emma blushes, something she only does when she's made a mistake or is embarrassed. Jace can read her well enough by now.

"No, I don't know him, and he hasn't contacted me personally. Why should he? But, there *is* something I have to tell you. It has nothing to do with the stones or our predicament. At least not directly," Emma beats around the bush, lowering her eyes. Jace bends down, catching her eyes from below.

"For God's sake Emma, WHAT is it?"

Emma sits upright, mustering her courage, eying Jace critically. Should she tell him? Is it the right moment? If not now…

Jace doesn't come from money like she does, but at the same time, she isn't sure he has the backbone to fight for what he loves. He's never been challenged in that respect. He grew up in a

Nottingham suburb inhabited by honest working-class families. His father was a foreman in a steel plant, worked his entire life there, earning himself a modest pension. They are steady, humble and retiring people. The pension is enough to get by on and his father is quietly proud of what he had achieved. Jace was a good student and his uncle had taught him to dive. For her part, she was brought up in circumstances two rungs up the ladder. Money was never an issue and she was an innocent when it came to the down and dirty of the streets. She was raised to believe in law and order, and should a misstep occur, one simply called the police and presto, things went back to normal. Jace was accustomed to keeping in the background, to lying low and keeping out of trouble. Is he strong enough? When he's gone from her and returns, her belly still does flipflops. She feels safe and content with him and from what she can tell, his family would welcome her with open arms. But will he be capable of protecting her and their child in this precarious situation?

After holding his eyes for some minutes without any sign of him beating a retreat, Emma announces, "I think I'm pregnant."

"What? How?"

"What do you mean how? Never heard of the birds and the bees?" Emma jokes, preparing to take him on. Jace puts their beer cans on the night table and makes ready for a counterattack.

"Maybe it's because I just can't keep my hands off you?" He grunts, grabbing her wrists and pressing them into the mattress. His face is so close to hers, her eyes so brilliant even out of focus. How beautiful she is!

"Are you sure?"

"Not completely, but my period is two weeks overdue. Do you want a child with me?"

Jace replies with a passionate kiss, his hands wandering beneath her sweater.

Emma giggles in his ear, "Just in case, huh?" and Jace slides her sweater over her head.

"It's amazing. I'm stunned…and thrilled," Jace whispers once they settle in the afterglow, swiping a sweaty strand of hair from her deeply flushed cheek.

"You're not afraid of being a papa? That's the end of our roving, you know," Emma says quietly, snuggling up to his side and holding him close.

Jace tugs on the blanket to cover them up but Emma's weight holds it down. She lifts herself enough to free the warm duvet and they settle beneath it in a tight embrace.

"Not at all! We're rich, we have endless options," Jace grins. Of course, he has doubts. A father? Does that fit into his plans? Sure. He has always wanted children, the chance to pass on what he feels is important to know about the world. But now? Yes! If not now, then when? Later, just later. But when later? What is the right time, are the ideal conditions for having a child? There is no clear answer. There probably isn't one anyway. Pregnancy happens and then you have to choose whether to accept it or not. It's that simple. People are no different than all other creatures on the planet.

If he could choose what to do with his life, he would want to be a biologist. That was the only subject in high school that had ever interested him. He would have liked to have studied, but the funds just weren't available. He had no choice in the matter. But he can now! Now, all the doors are open to whatever room he wants to enter. Why not follow his heart instead of putting all his eggs in one basket? Sure, diving is wonderful. Still, it's all about making choices, the same thoughts about having a child, just another dimension. A child is something fundamental, though. Where was he?

Yeah, the choice to procreate. Can it be that human beings are not so different from salmon? He's read a lot about salmon. Like human babies, no one asks them if they wanted to be conceived. Then they swim far out to sea, following an irresistible call to return to their place of birth. Maybe salmon also thought they were doing this willingly, procreating gladly. How does a female salmon choose her mate? Which criteria does she apply? How does the male choose her? Isn't this the same situation? Emma is pregnant and he has a choice to accept the child or not. So, what does acceptance mean?

Of course, this isn't a philosophical discourse on procreation. This is reality. It's about a child, his child. He's not a salmon. It's about commitment, to care for the child a lifelong. His lifelong. Ideally with the mother of his child, with Emma. That's the crux.

He's been together with Emma for several months now. According to his perspective, how long would he say they have been in a relationship? Jace tries to pin it down. Was it from the first time they slept together? Maybe. But then he would have been in many relationships with many different women. And that's certainly not the case. Was it when they began to share their dreams, to talk about the future, painting pictures that featured the two of them together? That's it! For him, that constitutes a relationship.

Jace is suddenly reminded of his father and what he had said to him when Jace was eight years old and wanted to have a dog.

Emma is watching Jace's face, a wide grin spreads from ear to ear as he travels far and wide in his thoughts. "What are you thinking about, Jace? Are you happy about the baby?"

Jace answers without a moment's hesitation, his eyes looking at a distant memory.

"I was just reminded of what my father said when I asked him if I could have a dog."

"A dog? Where's this coming from?" She asks, addled but grinning.

"Well, he explained to me that should I take on the responsibility for a dog, I would no longer be able to do what I liked whenever I wanted. That anything I wanted to do, I would have to consider my dog's welfare and plan accordingly. Besides, I would have to get up and go out with it every day, no matter what the weather."

"Hmm. You wouldn't have to take our child for a walk every morning, but you would have to change his or her nappies," Emma laughs, hugging him.

"No problem. I will want to, that's part of the program. And, yes, Emma, I'm looking forward to having a child with you. I've got a horde of butterflies, but it's a wonderful adventure!"

Emma snuggled up even closer to her man. Will her parents like Jace? They haven't met yet. When she told her mother that she had fallen in love with a colleague, there had been little enthusiasm. Of course, her mother conceded, living in such a close community created strong bonds, but Emma will only know if Jace is the right man after their Iceland adventure, when things took on an everyday routine. What she meant was that a man had to be reliable, have sown his wild oats before a woman could really know what she had and take the step to starting a family. Dependable, secure, constant. These three words were synonymous when her mum spoke about Emma's dad. But what constitutes Mr. Right for Emma? When it comes to raising children, Emma agrees with her mum. Will Jace be able to give up the gypsy life he loves so much? The diving? She hopes, no, she expects Jace to be a present and active father for their child. Reliable, consistent, there.

"We can arrange things any way we like. If we need a babysitter, we don't have to skip supper before the movie. We can pay for both. We're wealthy, Emma. We can give our children everything they need and still have time for ourselves. No scratching and scraping bye. Isn't that simply brilliant?"

Emma disentangles herself from his arms and sits upright. The money, the stones bring her back to their current reality and how this might affect their future together.

"Yes, it is, if we survive long enough to enjoy it. I don't want to spend my life on the run, Jace. Not with a child, not without one."

"Listen, if Chuck doesn't try to sell his ice, there's no need to worry. If he does, though, we're in deep shit."

"You're right. We need to get in touch with him and warn him," Emma remarks thoughtfully.

"You know Chuck. He's not going to give a damn about us or what we say but it's his life. How can that endanger us?"

"I don't know…but there's no way we can be sure. Maybe we should just give it all away. Get the stones from the lake and give them to Arik. Then it's over, really over."

Jace raises his head to get a good look at Emma.

"You're not serious, are you?"

"Of course not, we would still be accomplices of a sort, knowing where the diamonds were found."

"Huh! Glad to hear it! Do you have any idea how lucky we are? It's a veritable miracle that we're even alive! First, we barely escaped a volcano eruption, including out-running an avalanche. What a nightmare! And we walk away with a fortune in our pockets! And to top it all off, we're going to have child. Unbelievable! It's like a fairy tale except that we have much more than three wishes. We can do whatever we want!"

"And what do you want?" Emma asks with a sigh. Of course, Jace is right and evidence of his fighting spirit warms her heart.

For hours, they paint their future in the most brilliant and diverse colors, egging each other on to come up with the more radical, the more outlandish, the more ridiculous idea. They'll buy an island in the South Seas, home schooling their children and populate a paradisiac village, whole, healthy and innocent. They'll buy a farm in the south of England, grow organic foods and save their piece of the world. They'll sail the seven seas, living on their yacht, teaching their child to dive, discovering unknown miracles underwater. Laughing until tears roll down their cheeks, they are like children writing an endless list of wishes but can only choose one in the end. Emma's dreams are solid and practical, reflecting the world she knows, but a better one. Jace dreams of adventure, his ideas those of an endless vacation. Emma smiles to herself, I'll cure him of that, she thinks.

Dawn is breaking as they finally fall asleep. In the end, they agreed on the farm in their homeland. Actually, it was Emma who decided, bringing Jace around in the end. A beautiful house somewhere grand with enough land to keep horses and ponies. Nothing so big that tending it takes up all their time, but with plenty of space for family and friends to make extended visits. Not too isolated and not too far from the sea, so that Jace can go diving whenever he wants.

Another of Emma's ideas was an apartment in New York, but Jace said that would cost everything she had. He suggested spending half on their home and investing the other half to ensure a carefree life, only working when they felt like it. They should pool their funds, he suggested. Who was the practical one now? Emma raised her eyebrows questioningly and Jace crept from the bed to kneel down and propose, grinning like a fool. Emma had to laugh. He looked so funny, kneeling there naked, his unruly mane standing up every which way. What would her family say to such a proposal? She was a decent girl, you know. Jace tittered as he got back into bed and asked when the fine lady would grace him with answer? Eyes shining with joy, Emma didn't keep him waiting long.

As Emma lay breathing deeply beside him, Jace's mind was a whirlwind of thoughts. What an amazing life they would have! That is, if all went well over the next few days. And the days to follow.

TWELVE

"**D**ear Passengers, this is your pilot speaking. We will be landing in just a few minutes. Please fasten your seatbelts and accept our apologies in advance for the inevitable turbulence." More routine than sincere, but they've been warned.

Sam leans over Marie to look out the window, reminded of his arrival in Iceland not so very long ago.

Arik is sitting across from them, his personal employee – as he introduced him at the Bern airport – in the seat on his left. A silent man with angular features. No gorilla this one, like the man Arik sent the first time in Zurich. This man, he introduced himself as Igor, was a polished professional, well-mannered and not in the least immediately threatening. His reflexes, Sam noticed, were those of a martial arts adept. As Marie clamped her jacket under her arm to shake his hand, her cellphone slipped from the pocket. Igor's hand shot out and caught it, casually handing it back to her. He assured them he was there for their collective protection, imperceptibly nodding as he shook their hands. His English was colored with an East European accent. Beyond that, he had not said a word during the three-hour flight, yet Sam could feel his eyes observing him and Marie. He now nods at Sam to buckle his seat belt.

As the plane leans into the wind, Sam sees the Golf Stream's elegant curve emerge beneath the clouds where Iceland's shoreline meets the ocean.

They've been up and about since five o'clock. Marie made it perfectly clear he was not traveling to the find-site alone with Arik. She found it odd that Arik was not satisfied with GPS coordinates or a map. Why did they have to show him in person? Piet was all fired up to join Sam and Barbu was also more than willing. Emma and Jace, sleepily slurping their coffee on the bar stools in the kitchen, merely shrugged their shoulders when asked their opinion. On the way to the airport in the limousine Arik had sent, Marie remarked how unusually indifferent Emma and Jace seemed that morning. Something had changed. But Sam wasn't really listening. His thoughts were busy with Marie herself. He was surprised how insistent she had been, telling Piet and Barbu there was nothing to discuss. She, and none other, was going with Sam and she left the kitchen to put on the appropriate clothing. Sam had never seen her so determined, but this was not the place to talk about it. Though the glass between them and the driver was probably soundproof, it didn't mean he wasn't listening.

Sam is physically shaken from his thoughts. Once beneath the cloud-cover, the mighty winds buffet the sleek private jet from all sides. All four of them grip the sturdy armrests of their leather seats.

"Mon dieu," Marie whispers as they fly in a wide arc over Reykjavik. From where he's sitting, Sam only catches a glimpse of the city but judging by the looks on Marie and Arik's faces, he reckons little has changed. The northernmost European capital city still lies in rubble.

Drawing their anorak zippers up to the top and flipping the hoods over their heads, the foursome tramps from Keflavik Airport terminal to the heliport on the other side of the cracked tarmac. Gusting winds sweep puddles clear while the rain fills them again. Empty, full, empty, full.

In a matter of minutes, they are buckled into two rows of seats in the Jet Ranger that will take them to Þingvellir Park. Arik and Igor in front, Marie and Sam in back. Apparently, Arik has managed to organize every step of their way and Sam wonders just how many strings he had to pull to do so. Iceland is still under emergency rule. Obtaining a permit and fuel to fly, not to mention the helicopter itself, for other than strictly emergency purposes required powerful contacts.

With a wailing west wind, the copter lurches northeastward, persistently pushing its way toward Reykjavik, its rotors thwocking loudly. They rise and fall with each gust. The sky has cleared. The sun looks like it's been painted on a pale blue backdrop, wind tearing the few clouds to shreds. Delightful weather for Iceland although Sam knew it could change before you unzipped your jacket. It wouldn't surprise him if they met with sleet in the park.

Below them, the shambles that was once Reykjavik's Old City appeared. The tidal wave had reduced the colorful sturdy houses on the harbor to crude smears of paint on an artist's palette. The Harpa Concert Hall's resonating lights have been silenced; the glittering glass façade completely smashed. Asymmetrical, the steel girders hung empty of all content, as if first torpedoed then flooded and sucked clean by the undertow to be drowned in the harbor. A slew of giant excavators crawled through the chaos, scooping up debris and loading it onto trucks. The city's entire coastline up to the hill where the cathedral stands looks like it has been vehemently clawed by some other-worldly, mega-dimensional fingers scratching a mosquito bite. Orange construction lights are blinking everywhere. Marie and Sam notice that the coastal road had been provisionally patched and was now a solid double line of huge trucks, those loaded crawling toward the lava fields to dump rubble, those returning empty idling in the stop and go, waiting to be refilled. An endless, 24-hour cycle, drivers taking shifts to accelerate the clean-up. Marie points downwards and says something over the intercom. Sam hears her voice in his headphones but doesn't understand what she's saying. He leans over to see what she's pointing at from her perspective.

On the side streets leading to and from Hallgrímskirkja a hodgepodge of tables and chairs are set up, occupied by men, women and children sitting in the sun, drinking coffee or lemonade. Sam shakes his head, deeply impressed. He looks at Marie and sees the same emotions stirring her. The Icelanders are incredible! Surrounded by chaos and destruction, they have cleared a space to take their coffee in the sun. An endemic defiance taken for granted and Sam can easily imagine them sitting in the hot thermal pools discussing God and the state of the world.

Sam and Marie exchange tear-filled glances moved by these people's indomitable will to survive. What they are seeing is certainly not a sign of surrender or resignation. They accept Nature's power; her ability to wipe them from the face of the Earth, to crush them like so many beetles underfoot. And although surely every one of them has lost at least one friend or family member, life goes on and they intend to take part in it. Sam can't help but compare Iceland to Haiti where even now, ten years after the cataclysmic earthquake, very little has been re-built. The people live amid the rubble. Is it simply a matter of funds, of the millions more in aid that Iceland received without even asking? Or is it the innate mentality of the people that helps them cope with disaster? Perhaps generation upon generation of oppression, colonization and slavery instils an abysmal apathy while descendants of determined Vikings have no choice but to meet the challenge headlong. Sam's mind movie replays the last World Cup when ten percent of Iceland's population sat in the bleachers rooting for their underdog team, "Ho – ho – ho – ho," they chanted in unison, their primal power transforming the modern sports arena into an ancient battlefield.

Hallgrímskirkja cathedral glided past, standing on the hill, its audacious mass apparently untouched by Nature's fury. Leifur Eriksson, Iceland's discoverer and national hero, has been restored and replaced on his plinth, his stern, bronze face gazes once more over the horizon. Righting the fallen and broken statue was obviously a priority.

Sam wonders what became of Jon Friman, the hobby geologist. The last they saw of him he was high up on the cathedral's tower terrace where they had left him to make their way to the domestic airport. Jon was determined to document the disaster, and the shaky video on international news was certainly from his cell-phone. Still, they had heard nothing from him since.

A few minutes later, the cargo harbor comes into view. Many containers are still scattered about like Lego blocks or jut out of warehouse roofs like projectiles that failed to explode. More than half of their former home, V18, is nothing but pulverized rubble. Marie gasps, her hand on her mouth. There had been over sixty of them, Sam remembers, guides of all kinds – hiking, diving, climbing and more – and they had learned the fates of only a handful. Some had survived while on tour with clients, saving themselves and their wards.

Following the catastrophe, they took off, scattering in the four winds, finding their individual ways home. Of the diving team, only the managers Tara and Drake were still in the city, searching for survivors. Most of their employees had died disastrous deaths. Sam shudders. Ghastly. But the information they received was second, third and fourth hand, usually from Chuck's Icelandic friends. Sam feels shame wash over him. They have been so busy with their own troubles, they hadn't bothered to ask after those colleagues less fortunate, their true fates unknown. He steals a glance at Marie and sees his reproach mirrored in her flushed face. He promises himself he will start looking for them as soon as he's back in Switzerland.

The harbor and outer reaches are clogged with freight ships carrying aid supplies and building materials. On land, army trucks are lined up to receive the goods. British military uniforms swarm the area, attending to logistics.

With the wind now at their backs, the helicopter sweeps over the bay toward the park. As far as the eye can see, the landscape is covered with what looks like city snow after traffic has dirtied its purity. Ash rain has cloaked the Earth in toxic dust. They discover people below, shoveling the filth onto trucks, scratching their homes and gardens free with their bare hands.

Alongside a barnyard, Sam and Marie see Iceland ponies munching hay in small corral. What has happened to the herds of cattle in the barns? Under normal conditions, the meager Icelandic grassland is barely enough to satisfy the live-stock. Some farms are so large, they have to import feed for their animals. Although many are autonomous, supplying their own electricity with thermal generators to run milk machines, the dramatic lack of non-toxic hay or of access to imported feed has triggered emergency slaughter en masse. Poisonous slick has made the few fertile acres barren and the future prospects of Icelandic agriculture is grim indeed.

Sam's jaw drops as they fly over the place where Þingvallavatn Lake once encompassed over eighty square kilometers of clear, glacial water. Below them is nothing but a colossal, empty bathtub coated in brown slime. The earthquakes had opened unfathomable crevices between the tectonic plates, simply swallowing up the lake's waters. Silfra, beautiful, unique Silfra, is also gone. Where the canyon had nestled between the continental masses, gently fed by the nearby glacier, was now a tiny stream trickling down amid a huge expanse of slick and rocky debris.

The helicopter bends widely over the place where the Visitor Center once stood, giving a clear view of the valley. Sam remembers the many times he had driven over the winding road to and from Reykjavik. He can still see in his mind's eye the gentle green hills leading down to the coast. The shredded earth and mud-filled wounds that he now sees shake him to the core.

This is it. Here is the place that saved them from the tidal wave of ice and mud. Where Chuck drove them in the jeep, hellbent on getting to the slope upon which the radio antenna stood. Where they found the stones. And what if there's nothing left to find? There have been hundreds of after-shocks, fissures closed, others opened, entire slopes sliding into the valley. What if they don't find anything and Arik thinks they are playing him for a fool?

The chopper hovers over the concrete platform that held the antenna. The antenna itself lays bent over the chasm where earth had been wrenched from earth and hurled into the ocean. A part of the base is still anchored to the plinth, the rest limp and lifeless. Igor opens the door and without the slightest hesitation jumps down onto the platform, landing as gracefully as a cat. Arik tosses him a large sports bag and signals Marie and Sam to jump out, too.

Marie looks at Sam, skeptical. Jumping out of a swinging chopper is not her idea of a safe landing. The machine might be hovering steadily now, but it would only take one strong gust of wind the moment she jumps to send her into the abyss. Landing here was out of the question, though, and the longer she hesitates, the harder the jump will be. She slides from her seat out the open door. Igor catches her under her arms as if she were a Raggedy Ann doll and places her safely on her feet. Sam follows suit, stumbling slightly on the concrete plinth. Igor takes hold of his arm to steady him, immediately letting go, as if to signal to Sam that he trusts him to help himself. Beneath the thundering helicopter, Igor raises his hand and, with thumb and pointer forming a circle, asks Sam and Marie if they're all right. They respond in kind, noticing that Igor speaks diver's speak, too. Now, he circles his pointer finger, signaling the pilot who allows the helicopter to fall steeply before turning and vanishing in the direction of the Visitor's Center where there is plenty of space to land.

"Arik will wait for us there. He will return for us when we've finished collecting stones," Igor explains.

Now that the chopper's rotors are no longer pounding in their ears and their winds silenced, the devastating scene's atrocity slaps them hard. Marie's feet tingle as if she has just landed on the moon. Behind them, black, serrated lava fields stretch toward the city. In front of them, the rupture is kilometers long. The earthquake had shaken more than half of the mountain loose and the avalanche took it into the bay.

"You drove up here?" Marie's voice threatens to crack with incredulity.

"Yes. Jace knew of the turnoff and we just made it with the jeep," Sam points to the shards of washed concrete slabs still hanging onto reinforcement bars slithering down the abyss. "That was the road. It turned up at the last second and the avalanche swept past only a meter or two in front of us. Thanks to Chuck's demonic driving skills we're still alive."

"And that's when you found the stones and went back to Reykjavik on foot?" Igor asks in his guttural accent.

"Yes. There was nothing else we could do. Walking over the lava was torture! We were still in our diving suits and didn't have shoes. By the time we got to the coastal road, our feet were covered in cuts and the diving soles in shreds. But we made it, as you can see."

Igor gives a minimal nod and Marie is struck with awe as she stares at the brittle, sharp lava fields her friends had been forced to cross. Reykjavik is far away on the horizon. She could just make out orange blinking lights across from the bay. Sam edges over to the plinth's ridge and looks into the chasm.

"There, to the right of the antenna, see the scratch marks on the boulder?" Marie and Igor stand next to Sam, follow his finger and nod. "That's where…" Sam's voice cracked. An enormous knot in his throat keeps him from continuing. He clears his throat several times but cannot get the words out of his mouth.

It's as if it had just happened. The memory's vividness is a 3-D wide-screen shot projected onto his brain: Simi's eyes looking up to him in the fraction of a second before he fell with the jeep. Sam feels warm wetness coursing down his cheeks. Marie lays her hand on his shoulder and he looks into her saddened eyes. He pulls himself together.

"The jeep was hanging there before it slid over the edge, taking Simi with it."

Marie gasps and murmurs, "Poor Simi. Peace be on your soul. How could that happen?"

She sees Sam barely perceptibly shake his head and drops the subject.

Sam intentionally fails to mention that the reason why they couldn't save Simi, the true cause of his death, was the giant stone he refused to let go of, giving them his hand instead so they could pull him out in time. Sam couldn't say why. He thought Marie knew the story and Igor would hardly dredge the bay for the stone. Still, he senses it would be more prudent not to mention that a giant diamond is certainly down there somewhere. Maybe he just doesn't want Igor, and through him Arik, to know just how important the stones and their newly won wealth is to them. So important that one of them was willing to die for it. Such information would surely make them easier to manipulate, wouldn't it? And is it true? Are they all just as money-grubbing as Arik and his sort?

Sam shakes his head to clear his mind and points to the place where Simi and the jeep fell. Marie and Igor stare down to where his finger is pointing.

"You found the stones down there?" Igor asks tonelessly while Marie creeps closer to the edge, holding Sam's hand to keep her balance on the slick, muddy plinth. She looks down and can only shake her head.

Sam nods, answering Igor who opens the sports bag and withdraws rope and climbing harnesses. He draws one over his legs and tights the belts on his thighs, indicating Sam should don the other. He then fastens the rope tightly to the antenna base. Sam climbs into his harness and loops the rope through the rope clamp. Both men are now standing at the rim of the rupture.

Marie goes over to Sam and hugs him tightly, "Be careful," she whispers. Sam nods and takes a step over the edge while Igor lays the sports bag under the rope to protect it from abrasion. He then follows Sam into the crevice. The walls of the rupture crumble, toeholds simply falling away beneath their weight or their shoes skate over the slick coating of ash. Inch by inch, they take turns descending into the rupture, making sure they have enough space to maneuver should one of them fall. Sam scans the narrow fissures but sees nothing milky white. His hands are trembling, and his knees are weak, making it difficult to find his footing.

Although there is but a tiny trickle below in the abyss that was once softly rolling hills, the view horrifies him. Visions of the churning wall of mud and ice chasing them down like a predator distract him. He remembers the caravan and the children waving for them to stop, who were only seconds later devoured by the beast. No one would ever find even the smallest sign of them. They have been erased.

His subconscious screams, "Get out of here!" Urging him to halt his descent.

"You okay? Need help?" Igor calls down to Sam, annoyed at how slowly they are progressing. Sam merely nods, looking down for a place to put his foot.

"Left of your right foot," Igor instructs him, having a better view from above. Sam inches forwards on shaky legs, trying to concentrate on climbing. He tells himself the ropes are secured. That nothing can happen, and he needs to bring this nightmare to an end. Pull yourself together Samuel Frei! He shouts sternly in his mind. It works, and he continues moving downwards, step by step.

As he finally has solid rock beneath his feet, where the jeep was caught, Igor kicks loose a stone directly over Sam's head. He ducks just in time, but more stones follow, and he's struck in several places. Finally, the rain of rubble ceases. Igor is hanging in his harness and looks down at Sam.

"I'm okay, nothing dramatic," Sam pants and waves up to Marie who is peering over the edge with worry written all over her face.

Looking down, Marie forgets to breathe. Suddenly, a raging fury spreads like wildfire from her belly to her hair. If Sam were within reach, she would have slapped him several times in quick succession. What the hell is he doing? What are they doing here? Damn it to hell!

She bites her fist to keep from venting her wrath and realizes there is absolutely nothing she can do. The fierce fire slips from her stomach and turns to water in her gut, a gushing waterfall of fear. She fears for this man's life.

Stunned by feelings so utterly alien to her, by the emotions coursing through her body and mind, she realizes that it would be close to fatal for her if she loses this man. It would be like losing a limb. Marie shakes her head forcefully; the insight shakes her very foundations.

Now she knows. Clearer than anything she has ever known before. She wants Sam. She wants to share her life with him, her future. She wants him to be the WE in her life, from now until the end of their days. She is finished with just an I. She never again wants to miss the warmth and intimacy they share. This is such a new feeling, sharing equally the space in her body consumed with fear. A certainty and clarity that she has never felt in all her other relationships and lovers – not even a similar whisper. Is this what being in love is like? Her usually so accurate and sharp reason has no answer. She tries to shake off the insight. First off, Sam has to return to her in one piece. There will be enough time after that to consider this eccentricity of the heart. She discovers to her surprise that she's smiling from ear to ear. She feels so incredibly good. A whole new world opens up, lush and wonderful. Despite the precarious situation they are in, she is truly, unbelievably happy. She wants nothing but this man, taking all the accompanying fears and doubts into the bargain. She wants to hold onto this happiness, hold onto him for the rest of her life, knowing that nothing in this life is forever and changes will come. How in the world did this happen to her?

The sound of falling stones ceases.

"Sam?!" Marie shouts. Her voice echoes and she is struck by a spontaneous, surreal vision of calling Sam's name in an airport terminal where she is waiting for his arrival. She sees him coming toward her. She runs and jumps into his arms, kissing him as if she would swallow him whole. She giggles.

"Everything's fine Marie. Don't get too close to the ridge!" Sam calls back, concerned.

"Potomu chto – here, come up here," Igor calls down to Sam, pointing at a cleft nearby.

Sam laboriously scales the few meters to Igor. The slick surface offers him little purchase, so he has to use his muscle power, pulling himself up on the rope clip and bracing his body long enough to slip the clip higher. Panting and sweaty, he finally makes it back up to the narrow ledge where Igor is standing.

Igor points to a tight crevice about two meters to the side, and there, below them, Sam now sees the white stones. Igor releases his rope clip and edges around Sam to try and secure himself below him. Sam shakes his head. It's insanely risky. But before he can stop him, Igor is already beneath him, holding onto Sam's thigh and reattaching his rope clip onto the rope.

With an assassin's dispassion, Igor calmly climbs over Sam. Sam could easily imagine him pulling the trigger, checking his victim's pulse and walking away. Job well done. Igor is not paying the slightest heed to his own safety, nor to Sam's. He has a job to do. A job he was trained for, honed and polished. His teachers had probably convinced him he was born for just such situations. This man is of an utterly different caliber than the gorilla Chuck duped and killed. Apparently, Arik has increased his investment, unwilling to take any more risks. What would he do if a man like Igor turned up at his home, threatening his family? He's as cold as ice and Sam shivers. But then he sees the glint in Igor's eyes as he views the stones. The same glint in Simi's eyes and Sam tenses. Greed defeats reason again. How is this going to play out?

Igor reaches into the fissure and holds up one of the stones to the light, assessing it with his mouth half-open.

Sam has the sensation of being caught in a time-warp. Simi, Igor, Igor, Simi. With Igor, however, the transformation is even more grotesque. A calculating, well-bred, self-contained and polished surface veneered a ruthless exactitude. At least it did. Within seconds Igor's brain has rewritten his entire biography and possible futures. All the things he had never dared to dream now seem within reach, flooding his consciousness with im-possibilities suddenly possible. Just as it had been with Simi. A new, self-determined life where any-thing goes, as long as it's what he wants. His brain receptors are chock-full of dopamine, serotonin and whatever other stimulators. Igor feels invinci-ble. He's Iron Man.

Seconds that feel like hours. Igor finally shakes himself and snorts, nodding several times, satis-fied. Not because he has fulfilled his mission, Sam is certain of that. There is more than aloof content in Igor's eyes. All the same, he has himself back under control.

The stone in his hand vanishes into Igor's pocket and he reaches back into the fissure, col-lecting stones. He joggled at the ridge of the crack to widen it. Damn! Not so well under con-trol. Like a dog with his teeth clamped onto one end of a bone that someone is trying to take from him, Igor growled, stemming his feet into the nar-row ledge and pulled violently on the loosened stone.

"Leave it!" Sam cries out in frustration. "It's too precarious! You've found the stones. Now you know where they are!"

Igor ignores him and slides his rope clip a bit higher, bracing himself and kicking at the soil with his hiking boots. The earth slides downward and away from them. Igor takes a step into the now wider fissure. The moment his weight rests on the left foot, the slope he was standing on slides away. He falls into the rope, jerking Sam nearly off his feet and he hears a sharp cry from above. Marie is beside herself with fear. Sam manages to right himself, but with Igor swinging below, he is also swaying in the rope. Then he sees the rope below him and above Igor is caught on a lave ridge, shaving into the nylon fibers with each swing of the rope. Sam can see the tiny ends curling away from the core. Three or four more swings and the rope is cut clean. Igor registers the danger and clamps all fours against the rock to stop the swaying. It works. He pulls himself up on the rope to the fissure's ridge but his clip catches on the raveled rope. Sam watches in horror as Igor lets go with one hand, removes the clip and replaces it above the damaged section of rope. The man's nuts! Sam only wants to get up and out of there. He longs to go home, wishing he had never seen anything resembling a diamond. Since they found the stones, his life has been threatened every other day.

Taking extreme care and effort, they inch their way up to the concrete platform. Sam is exhausted, bathed in sweat. Igor shows them one of the stones. His hands are covered in dirt and blood. Blood is also oozing from scratches on his face and the knees on his pants are dyed dark red. It seems the diamonds have not only robbed him of reason, they have also rendered him oblivious to pain.

"You told the truth, old man, there really are raw diamonds in the lava. There's probably tons of them in this mountainside," he murmurs.

"How beautiful you are, my dear," Igor whispers, gazing at the stone like a smitten teenager, drool dribbling from the corner of his mouth.

Sam shakes his head in disgust. "Well, did you think we made up the story? Maybe we stole the raw diamonds from a demolished jeweler's in Reykjavik?" Sam asks angrily, watching Marie's face. She's as hypnotized by the stones as everyone else is. Just like when they stumbled over them the first time. Now she knows, too, where the stones came from. One more player on their team. But Marie's mind movie is playing a different film than Sam assumes. It's not the stones that captivate her, it's the thrill of danger involved in attaining them. Aside from the seven of them, only Igor and Arik know where the treasure is buried.

"Now we know for certain," Igor comments drily, slipping the stone back into his pocket and pulling out the walkie-talkie from his jacket. His training and brain-washing are back in control. The job was to find proof of the stones' origin and that he has done. For a man like him, probing any further would be fatal. He's one of the best in his field and recognizing his limits is the only chance he has of growing old. Or knowing the right time to call it quits.

Marie follows the hand with stone to the pocket. Sam looks at her, addled. Her eyes are large and dark, but the glimmer is gone. There is only warmth and relief, no fierce lust for more. Is she as happy as he is that they are done here?

Hours later, Marie and Sam are traipsing over the Bern Airport tarmac, making for the terminal. It's after midnight and they're back where they were almost twenty-four hours ago.

When they had landed the helicopter in Keflavik, Marie announced her intention to stay in Iceland. She wanted to look for Jon and find out what she could about others' fates. Arik had no objections, but Sam wanted to get home. He couldn't wait to escape the island, the chaos and destruction. Not only that, if they did stay – Sam wasn't about to leave Marie behind – when they had had enough and wanted to go back, finding a flight home would be nearly impossible. They would have to take a ship and several train rides before they got to Switzerland. They had already done that once, did Marie really want to do it again? Hearing the facts, Marie changed her mind. Before they lifted off from Keflavik, Sam went to the toilet. On his way back, he observed Marie speaking to Arik. He saw Arik stroke her arm, saw Marie nod at what he was saying and then they shook hands. Nothing suspicious. But Marie's reaction when she saw Sam coming gave him pause. She immediately stepped away from Arik, combing her hair with her fingers nervously. She then gave him a smile to die for, threading her arm through his and plappering about the horrid weather in Iceland and if the weather in Switzerland would be nicer? Sam refrained from asking what she was talking to Arik about and what their apparent agreement entailed. He had the impression the two were acquainted with one another but as far as he knew, they had only met yesterday.

He wondered if he was getting paranoid. Had the stones and the wealth they brought turned his head? Maybe Arik had only ensured her that their troubles were now over and shook her hand to confirm it. Sam doesn't know what to believe and he's worried that if he mentions what he thought he saw with Chuck a few days ago and now his suspicions about Arik, he'd wind up making a fool of himself in front of Marie. She might just get wind of his suspicions, see just what an old, jealous man he is and leave him. The thought made him cringe. He just couldn't risk it.

How depressing! Hasn't he come an iota further? Is his fear of loss still so much more powerful than his need for clarity? So, what if he suspects Marie is possibly double dealing him? That's part of who he is, and it'll come out eventually anyway. But he loves this woman, even if it means his ruin. And the fact is, he's not above suspicion himself. His doubts could just as well arise from his lack of self-confidence, from old wounds. Maybe it's all in his mind. Sam sighs heavily.

An hour or two later, they're sitting in the living room in Sam's house, nipping their nightcaps. Emma and Jace are still up, eager to hear how things went. Barbu is at the bar mixing drinks and making sandwiches. Marie asks where Piet might be, he's always so eager to know everything, has he already gone to bed? Emma shakes her blond curls sadly.

"What's up?" Sam asks.

"Well, it's kind of weird. This afternoon, Piet packed his things and took a train. We aren't even sure where he went," Jace tells him, his voice low, his expression confused.

"Without saying goodbye?" Marie cries out incredulously.

"I think he got a call from home, maybe a friend, I don't know. He didn't want to tell us," Emma answers.

"And then he just left?"

"Yeah. He was suddenly at the door with his bag and said he wasn't much for long goodbyes. We should give his love to you both and he'll be in touch," Jace relates.

"That's odd," Sam remarks.

"Yeah, it is, but what can you do? He'll call, I guess. Now tell us how it went," Barbu interjects, taking a sandwich and passing the plate around. Enough riddling about Piet.

Marie tells them about the devastation they found on Iceland, so much ruined! But she also describes the energy and determination so evident among the people there. And, yes, they found the diamond vein again and Arik told her they were free and clear, as long as they didn't do anything rash. This annoys Emma to no end. When Marie has finished her narrative, they are all suddenly exhausted and wish for nothing but their beds. As they rose to go behind their separate doors, Emma announces, "There is something I want to tell you…" Barbu is already in the hallway, on his way to the bathroom and comes back, resuming his seat on the sofa.

The three of them sit and gaze expectantly at Emma, who smiles sheepishly. So, it's good news, Sam thinks, smiling back at her. Emma hems and haws until Marie asks, "What is it sweetie, have you won another million in the lottery? Come on, tell us!"

Emma snorted with laughter, shaking her head, "Sure, that's all I need, more money problems!"

"Oh, Emma!" Barbu puts in amid the general laughter, "If you are having trouble getting rid of your money, I'll gladly volunteer my help."

"No, it's something completely different…" Emma continues, sobering. She crosses over to Jace and takes his hand and announces softly, "I think I'm pregnant. Jace and I have decided to go back to England and settle down. Our gypsy days are over. We're going to start a family."

Barbu's customarily melancholy expression lights up. Smiling broadly, he goes to Emma and wraps her in an enthusiastic hug then turns to Jace, giving him a playful slap on the cheek before laying his forehead on Jace's, murmuring, "Congratulations, my friend. I am so happy for you, truly I am."

Sam looks at Jace, trying to keep his doubts from his face. An anchored Jace? Hard to imagine. Still, Sam shouts, "Wow!"

Marie sets herself next to Emma and pulls her close. Sam examines Jace's face smiling back at him and nodding bashfully. At least he intends to leave the roaming life behind, Sam concedes. But how long is that going to last?

"And when are you planning to leave?" Sam asks, "I mean when can we visit you? Is there going to be a wedding?"

"We haven't set the date yet but keep an eye on your mailbox!" Jace says with a wink at Sam.

"You just have to visit us! We're looking for a nice, simple farmhouse. Comfortable with space for you all! I want to try my hand at breeding ponies and, and," Emma's cheeks are flushed with excitement.

"You can bet your life I will come! We'll chatter on about the good old days and our adventures," Marie says, hugging Emma again and again.

She didn't say *we'll* come Sam thinks sadly. It seems they are all readying to leave and begin their new lives, a thought that makes him more than blue. For a few weeks he had felt a part of something, he felt he belonged. He had made friends and found a woman he loved and thought she felt the same. Was it only the riches? Or would they have eventually gone their separate ways anyway, regardless of what had transpired on Iceland? No drama, no diamonds, no clash with the syndicate? Probably. After all, he was almost old enough to be their father and when he was their age, he wouldn't have befriended someone his age. It would have seemed strange. Still, they have had intense moments of deep intimacy over the last weeks. But maybe that is only his perception. He still can't muster the courage to ask Marie about her true feelings toward him.

He gazes blindly at the tiny red and white lights on the lake's far shore, barely hearing Mare and Emma's excited talk about family and children. No one seems disposed to go to bed anymore. Barbu and Jace are talking about diving and all the places they have yet to see but will certainly go to at some point.

Sam feels the weight of his years. He's so tired. He should be happy. He has enough money to last out his life. He will never have to take on one of those unspeakably boring jobs again. He's as free as a bird, can go wherever he wants, do whatever strikes his fancy. Maybe work as a diving instructor, just for fun. But where's the fun? Won't he just up and run when things get difficult? Why should diving be any different? He doesn't need the money. He will never have to answer to anyone again and that's the rub. He feels bereft. No matter how difficult it had been at times, the chase, the hunt, the challenge had always been his source of strength, had always given his life meaning.

Soon, Barbu will take his leave, too. And then his future with Marie will be decided. But who is he kidding? It's obvious. There won't be one.

As usual, he paints his future as pessimistically as possible. Things can only go uphill from there.

THIRTEEN

Marie and Sam are enjoying the sunshine at the small sidewalk café directly behind the East Interlaken train station. Barbu went out after breakfast to explore the hills. Yesterday, they were here with Emma and Jace, having a last cup of coffee before the two of them boarded the train to Calais.

Jace and Emma had decided on taking the land and sea route to England. The prospect of trying to explain two million Swiss francs in their bags to airport security led them to booking train tickets to France. With British passports, the probability of luggage control on the train was about one in a zillion, at least until they boarded the ferry in Calais. To avoid any baggage control at all, Jace asked a friend of his to pick them up in his trawler at a small jetty close to Calais and ferry them across to his home harbor, Dungeness. And not even the British Coastal Police would think of searching two young people dressed in oilskins on a fishing boat. Especially not one that came and went regularly. His friend asked no questions. Why should he? He is a friend. Jace offered to pay for fuel and that was that. Sam felt the plan was good.

Saying their goodbyes on the train platform, both Sam and Marie expressed their joy for the young couple heading home, eager to explore their new life together. Sam nearly felt encouraged enough to ask Marie about their own future together but, as always, he changed his mind. The moment the train left the station, Marie became very quiet and when he asked her what was on her mind, she said she didn't envy Emma and Jace.

In her opinion, leaving home for something new and different was much easier than returning home and trying to find your place amidst familiar surroundings. She was certainly going to miss Emma, but her mind was more on her and Jace's problems than on their prospects of a happy future together. Sure, they will have some hurdles to take, that's how life works, Sam replied. In any case, considering Marie's gloomy forecast for their friends' burgeoning family, Sam didn't think this was the right moment to talk about their own, possible future.

When he asked Marie if she held high hopes for the young family, her laconic response was, "Only time will tell." He took her in his arms, and they strolled back to his house, each preoccupied with their own thoughts. They might have taken a walk along the shore, but Barbu was waiting at home.

He carried his grief well, but they still didn't want to leave him alone for too long with only his thoughts for company.

Without looking up from the blog he's reading on his cellphone, Sam navigates his cappuccino toward the table. Suddenly, his senses catch something out of the ordinary. What now? He yearns for a taste of normalcy, just taking a cup of coffee at the local café, enjoying the summer sun. There's been very little of it in their lives lately.

Sam shifts his gaze to the crowd of chattering Chinese pulling their wheelie cases and gathering about their guide. Since air traffic has resumed, crowds of Asians once more fill European airports and train stations. Nothing unusual. Although rather small, the train station is a busy one. Interlaken is the launching pad for Alpine excursions and shopping tours of the city's renowned watchmakers. Over the past few years, he has seen more and more Chinese tourists here. Same ole, same ole. Soothing monotony. Sam is about to return to his reading when he sees what turned up on his radar.

Suddenly on guard, Sam stares over Marie's head, bent over her mobile reading with the sun's warmth on her back. His eyes rest for a moment on her shape as she absently twists a lock of her hair around her finger as she scans the news over the rim of her sunglasses, her thumb scrolling down the display.

Sam looks back at the man climbing the stairs from the underpass beneath the tracks amid a swarm of tourists. He's coming their way. Combat boots, cargo pants, over-sized sunglasses, wool cap, and duffel bag, his tall, stocky form sticks out in the crowd of Asians. Sam thinks he recognizes that earth-eating stride and shameless grin.

Unsettled, he wonders if he is seeing things. What is Chuck doing here? Why is he coming back? Sam swallows and tries to breathe down his discomfort. What's going on? His thoughts are running away with him.

"Have you heard anything from Chuck lately?" Sam asks Marie without taking his eyes off the approaching figure.

Marie slides her sunglasses down to the tip of her nose and gives Sam an irritated glance.

"Why do you ask me that? It's the third time since he's been gone! Are you jealous or something? If I had talked to Chuck, I would have told you!"

"Hmm," Sam grunts as the Chuck approaches their table. His eyes on Sam, he places his finger on his lips. No need. Sam is speechless anyway, couldn't speak if he wanted to.

"Really, chérie, what is the problem?" Marie lays her cellphone the table and sets her sunglasses on her head, raising her hands in supplication or invitation, nodding as if she could thusly lure the words from his mouth. He doesn't even look at her, but over her head as if his thoughts are somewhere else.

There's something come between us, I just know there is, Marie thinks. The steady intensity of their union is showing signs of stagnation, but she cannot find the culprit blocking the flow. Sometimes, when she touches his naked skin, she feels as if she's caressing a neoprene suit. There is an inexplicable distance between them as if Sam has donned some kind of armor and Marie cannot find the latches to open it. At first, she thought he was simply retreating for a while from all that they had been through, a respite to gather new strength now that their troubles were over. But then Sam had begun to ask her odd questions, mentioning Chuck. She had told him everything about her short affair with Chuck before she fell for Sam, hoping to bridge the gap. Still, Sam remained distant. Initially, the schism saddened her, but eventually it only annoyed her. Initially, she was angry at herself. You silly thing, she railed, did you really believe you had found someone to whom you could completely surrender? Trust! She is a fool and always will be. That moment of absolute clarity she had had in Iceland as Sam and Igor climbed over the ridge. It was the thrill, the danger, not love! But now, when he asks again, she senses the hot knot in her belly loosening and spreading its heat upwards, catching in her throat. She swallows hard to keep from screaming at him. She knows she won't be able to keep it in much longer. But then she sees Sam's eyes flick over and behind her. Just as she moves to turn around, two strong, callused hands close over her eyes.

"Coucou, my lovely! You have three guesses. And to help you out, it's not Santa Claus," a voice behind her ear murmurs, followed by a braying laugh.

"Chuck!" Marie cries out, sweeping his hands from her eyes and jumping from her chair.

Sam watches Marie hug Chuck, patting him on the back, thrilled to see him, jumping up and down like a little girl. Her sadness and anger flip seamlessly into joy and enthusiasm. One second she's ready to read Sam the riot act, the next she's giggling happily. Tears course down her cheeks, and she doesn't know which emotion brought them about, her vanishing anger or her happiness at seeing Chuck. Apparently, hopping about helps her process the roller-coaster of feelings. Sam watches the reunion. Chuck pushes his sunglasses up and winks at Sam, grinning over Marie's shoulder. Sam pulls a cigarillo from his shirt pocket, tamps it on the table and lights up. His first impulse is to jump up and join the Chinese, escaping to some tourist attraction. Just gone. He searches his mind for reasons why Chuck has suddenly turned up again. Has he come for Marie or is there something more sinister motivating him? Sam can't just chalk up this feeling to jealousy. He grins warily, but Chuck doesn't seem to notice, and Marie probably just thinks he's jealous. Or she couldn't care less either way.

Chuck swings his duffel bag onto the ground next to the free chair and straddles the seat. He waves to the waitress, mouths 'beer' with his hands measuring a large glass. Halfway to their table, the woman nods and makes an about-face back inside. Chuck acts as if he has only been around the corner and is looking forward to a merry evening among friends. I'm here; let's celebrate!

Marie plucks at her clothes and musses her hair as she always does when she's excited. She opens fire, literally bombarding Chuck with questions about how he's doing, where he's coming from, why he's here and what he's been up to, interspersing the attack with exclamations on how happy she is to see him. Sam observes the two of them, how Marie tucks her chair next to Chuck's, her hand on his shoulder, playing fondly with his hair.

Chuck answers each question with his obnoxious laugh. He condescendingly places his hand on Sam's knee. "It's good to see you lovebirds," he comments, winking first with one then the other eye at Sam. Marie pinches his cheek. His beer arrives, and Marie hops her chair back to give the big man room. Chuck takes a long pull from his beer, wipes the foam from his lips and sighs loudly, "Delish! Boy, am I glad to be here! What luck to meet up with you two here!" Marie's the only one sharing his enthusiasm, her eyes shining and fixed on his face. Sam is far from glad.

But he finally remembers his manners and stretches out his hand. The two men grip thumbs and hands. Making contact, Sam believes he can read in Chuck's eyes that he isn't here for Marie. At least he thinks he isn't. But why then?

Chuck reads his thoughts and begins to tell them his story. He had been back home, had met up with old friends, but nothing was like it used to be. He was bored. Had made a few tentative attempts to sell the stones, but it soon became clear that this was not going to be easy. When he had finally arranged a meeting with a possible buyer, it turned out that it was Arik sitting in the limo, or least he thought it was when he scanned out the meeting place with his binoculars. It's a bloody mess, that's what it is and brayed his trademark laugh.

"And now?" Sam asks in a cautiously conciliatory tone. He sees trouble on the way. Chuck's presence will only make his confrontation with Marie more difficult. That is, if he really is here because of the diamonds and the money.

Marie smiles and strokes Sam's cheek. Such a small gesture and his tension loosens a bit. What does he want? Chucks seems to read his thoughts.

"Now, it's like this, I have the ice in my bag and would like to trade them in for my share of the cash. It's that simple."

"You're incredible! And how do you propose we do that? Piet is in Holland, Jace and Emma in England. Barbu's still here, but anyway. Are you going to turn up at their doors and demand your cut?" Sam exclaims, doing his best to keep his tone friendly.

"Hmm," Chuck mutters. "I didn't know everyone had already hit the road. That complicates matters, but you can't deny I have a right to my cut."

Sam looks at Chuck sharply and shakes his head, grinning. As soon as one problem's solved, another one turns up. Chuck is Chuck – an incorrigible egomaniac! You either have to love him or hate him, there's no in-between. He's like marmite, that yeasty English bread spread. You either can't get enough or it makes you want to puke. That's how it is with Chuck the pit bull. He shows up out of nowhere and puts his game marker in the front as if that's the way of the world.

Still grinning, Sam can't decide which it is – does he hate him or love him?

Chuck interprets Sam's shake of the head as a turndown. He raises his eyebrows.

"No, Chuck, don't get me wrong. Of course, you're entitled to your share. It's just not that easy anymore. Need I remind you, that you were the one who chose to decline your part of the money and take off with the large stone on your own?"

Chuck takes a breath to respond, but Marie cuts him off, "The important thing is that you're here," she mediates, "we'll find a solution." Smiling, she places one hand on his knee and the other on Sam's.

"I'm not here to see you," Chuck cuts her off brusquely, "I'm here for the money."

Marie's eyes widen in astonishment, looking at Sam, "That's not how I understood it!" Understood what? Sam wonders what she means. Was she referring to their reunion a moment ago, or did she know he was coming? He feels his chest tightening, his stomach turning.

"Easy, Marie. I didn't mean it like it sounded. I'm broke, and you guys are swimming in cash. We need to figure this out and then I'm on my way again," he grumbles in appeasement and adds a hee-haw, his habitual method of reasserting his territorial rights.

"And you have just the idea," Sam states more than asks.

"Sure…"

Sam shows his open palm, "Let's hear it."

But its Marie who answers. "We can get the small stones from the lake and deposit the big one in the net. The small stones are easy to sell." The knot in his chest spreads behind Sam's eyes, his temples thrumming. He's a breath away from screaming. Damn! Just who does he think he is? He turns up and expects everyone to jump to do his bidding, regardless of the possible perils involved. Sam looks up into the cloudless sky, counting to ten in his mind.

"Okay, we could do that," Sam yields, "but how are you going to distribute them among people spread out all over Europe?" he asks. The endless diamond nightmare churns to life, but he's determined to stay cool.

"If I remember correctly, we had six bags of stones. I'll take one of them and that's that," Chuck says with a grin, waving his hands is if to fan down Sam's heat.

Marie raises both arms. Evidently, for her, the problem's solved.

Sam can't shake the feeling that he's not just negotiating with Chuck, but with Chuck and Marie both. He copies Marie's gesture and watches the smoke from his cigarillo rise and dissipate on the warm summer air until there is nothing left to see. He's tempted to just get up and go home, pack his money and drive off in the jeep. Let them see how far they get shoveling their own shit. It wouldn't be the first time he had fled chaos in this manner. He'd done it often and it had worked perfectly. When the dust has settled, he'll come back home, readjust his plans and go on with his life. He'll find out then how they had handled the situation. He wonders if they'll leave his house standing or burn it to the ground before they took off for wherever. And even if everything ended in disaster – it would end. Maybe it's time to start out on a new life anyway. Again. He grins at the thought.

The only thing holding him back is the woman sitting across from him. Evidently sniffing out his escape plans, she flings her arms around his waist and lays her head on his shoulder. Life is so irrational! A few months ago, he didn't even know of this Frenchwoman's existence, would neither have desired nor missed her. Now he thinks he can't live without her! What balderdash! What can he do? She's here now and he will never be able to forget her, even if he wished he could right now. The rest of his life will be haunted by the depth and intensity of their unity, the profound awareness of his capacity to love, even when it's more than likely that he will be left with nothing but the memory.

FOURTEEN

Barbu lifts the full tanks onto the boat's bench and begins fastening the buoyancy devices and screwing on the diving regulators.

They had spent the entire afternoon lamenting Chuck's idiocy. It had been his idea in the first place to take a big stone and get out of Dodge, laughing up his sleeve at the rest of them, thinking he had made the better deal. Now that they had finally gotten Arik and his thugs off their backs once and for all, he has to turn up and cause a new kind of trouble.

It was Barbu who finally soothed Sam's jangled nerves by reminding him that if it wasn't for Chuck, they wouldn't be here to have any problems. Sure, Chuck's a pain in the ass but the solution isn't such a bad one. One more diving tour and it's over. Gagging his inner voice, Sam reluctantly agreed. But it wasn't Barbu's reasoning that convinced him, it was Marie. Like a Siamese twin, she stuck to his side, making it unmistakably clear to whom she belonged. A small voice in Sam's mind persisted in smelling a rat but the intimacy Sam had so missed was louder. He dismissed the thoughts plaguing him over the past week, wrote them off as jealous suspicion. He told himself it was his brooding that was driving Marie away, he doesn't blame her. While Barbu was off for a walk and Chuck taking a nap, Sam took the opportunity to apologize to Marie. She didn't even ask for what, she knew that he was the cause of the sudden aloofness between them. She simply took both his hands and led him to the bedroom. Sam was grateful for the renewed intimacy.

Humans are truly astonishing creatures. What words can never achieve is so easily rectified when the body is permitted to lead the way. Skin on skin, warmth, caresses and the smell of intimacy. Nothing is more honest or more communicative. Words, discussions, explanations are utterly useless in comparison. Messages sent with a smile or kind words are so easily misconstrued, but a touch speaks from the heart and the body never lies. All at once, they found each other again, their merging was a home-coming and unmistakable. Everything felt right, even later, as the four of them were eating dinner on the terrace, discussing and agreeing on their plan. They would dive that very night.

Under a light rain trickling down from a low, moonless sky, Chuck and Sam are donning their dry suits. Cradled in polished water, their navigation lights doused, the boat lies motionless directly alongside the cliff wall. They had waited until nightfall to load and untether the boat, paddling far out on the lake before Marie started the motor. Quietly blubbering, they glided over the water, a dark shadow merging with the dark night.

With a soft splash, Chuck and Sam vanish beneath the black surface, gently falling side by side, checking their instruments and adjusting buoyancy to compensate for the increasing pressure. The vertical rock wall glides past them, as if it is the mountain moving and not them. Sam sees the small sack dangling from Chuck's vest. He has brought the large diamond in exchange for a baggie-full of small ones. As they paddled across the lake, Sam had made his decision. This endless carousel they're riding must come to a halt. Only when the stones have vanished from their lives, will they cease to believe there is even more money to be had. No more wrangling, no more perfidious thoughts slithering into their minds and poisoning their relationships. And no more worries about the syndicate! No stones, no greed. Arik knows where they found the diamonds and when he also knows the divers have lost any they might have had, there's a very good chance they can put a period at the end of this episode. They should be thankful for what they have and get on with their lives. Sam is fully aware that Chuck, Marie, Barbu and the others would never agree to his plan. They would be furious if they knew. But if he doesn't tell them and makes the loss look like an accident, what can they do? They'll get over it one day and most likely even thank him!

They discover the small ledge in the wall and Sam checks his device – thirty-two meters. This is it. He points to the two steel cables anchored to the wall with pitons and carabiners and glides his finger downward to the nylon bag the apparatus is holding. Chuck swims to the carabiners while Sam kneels on the ledge and draws the nylon bag up in front of him. He places the bag on the ledge and Chuck unhooks the carabiners, so Sam can loosen the cable and open the bag.

Chuck then joins Sam on the ledge. For moment, Sam follows the bubbles of his breath, losing them quickly in the blackness. As agreed, Marie and Barbu are drifting slowly in darkness, with neither position lights nor the stern spotlight. Sam can only hear the gentle hiss of his and Chuck's breath.

Chuck opens the nylon net, unhooks the small bag on his vest and places it deep in the cache. He takes out the baggies with small stones and sorts them on the ledge. He chooses one and puts the others back, examining his choice in the light of his lamp. The nylon net is behind him on the edge of the ledge. Now's his chance!

Sam calmly places three large lake rocks in the bag and zips it closed. He shoves the weighted bag to the edge and hesitates a second too long.

Chuck grabs his shoulder and shakes him hard. Angry wet sounds explode from Chuck's regulator in a whirlpool of bubbles. Chuck wrests Sam's mask from his face and the regulator from his mouth. Suddenly blind and without air, Sam tries in vain to wrench himself free from Chuck's iron hold. Shocked, Sam realizes that Chuck isn't intent on keeping him from sinking the bag. Chuck is trying to kill him. Terror and adrenaline course through his body in hot waves. Sam writhes in panic, but Chuck has him clasped tightly against his body. Sam gropes along Chuck's hip, his fingers searching for the zipper's tab. The second his fingers grip metal, Sam jerks hard downwards. Icy water floods Chuck's suit and he releases Sam to close it again, his legs already going numb. Sam reels away and catches a blurred glimpse of the bag on the lip of the ledge. With a powerful kick, his flipper sends the bag sliding over the rim and into the depths.

With a single flipper-stroke, Chuck is at the steel cable slithering swiftly after the sinking bag. The lake floor is over two hundred meters below and he knows once the treasure hits bottom, he will never be able to find it again, let alone retrieve it. He snatches the cable with one hand and Sam follows the quivering lamplight into the deep, since even Chuck must succumb to gravity.

Chuck pays no mind to his computer's beeping alarm. Sinking rapidly, he swallows hard several times to compensate for the rising pressure on his ears. He pulls on the steel cable until he has the bag of diamonds in his arms. He clasps it close to his body with one arm as if it would save his life instead of plunging him to perdition. He presses the button on his vest to compensate the weight Sam added to the bag. Air floods the vest, buoyancy decelerating and gradually stopping his fall. His vest fully inflated, Chuck is suspended by the wall, clutching the bag. His diving computer tells him he's at fifty-one meters. Much too deep! At this depth and pressure, large portions of the natural carbon in his breath will be pressed into his bloodstream like a household carbonation machine for making bubbly water.

He has to rise soon to avoid saturating his blood with the deadly gas, otherwise he will be

forced to make decompression stops to safely surface. If he doesn't, his blood will begin to froth,
like a coke bottle shaken before opening. But the
air level in his tank will not allow a slow, careful ascent with decompression stops. He has to rise,
fast!

Furious, he bellows into his air regulator. One
end of the steel cable is tangled in the gear behind him while the other hangs loosely in front,
obstructing his legs and flippers. He doesn't dare
open the bag and jettison the weighty stones.
What if he dumps the diamonds in the process?
He quickly decides to slip out of his vest and the
firmly fastened tank, pull them to his front and un-
tangle the cable so he can move freely again. It's a
common diving maneuver and any instructor
worth a damn can do it blindly. The trick is not to
lose the inflated vest and send it rocketing to the
surface without him in it. He presses the valve reg-
ulating the pressure in his suit. Air flows in forcefully but fails to drive out the icy water surrounding
his legs. Already, the cold is limiting his lung-
power, his breath shallow. Soon, he will begin to
stiffen and lose control over his limbs. He must
surface quickly. The added buoyancy in this suit
sends him upwards and again Chuck ignores his
computer's warning. He's rising too fast, inviting
the risk of ebullition where the pressurized air in

his blood makes bubbles and blocks his arteries. The result would have the same effect as a heart attack compounded by several consecutive strokes.

His teeth clamped tightly on the air regulator's mouthpiece attached to the tank anchored on the vest, Chuck wrestles with the steel cable, trying to uncoil it from his gear. He has only one arm free as the other is still pressing the bag of diamonds to his chest. And that's how it happens. The vest slips from his hand and shoots upwards, tearing the air regulator from his mouth. The sudden upraise also rips out the hose supplying his suit with pressurized air, his only other connection with the vest. The entire rig, including his air supply, zooms up and away to the surface.

Chuck begins to sink again, his suit's buoyancy impotent. It may have supported Chuck but was outweighed by the stones' load. His diving calculator displays twenty-three meters. Twenty-four, twenty-five. He has to choose! Almost tenderly, he relaxes his arm and in no time the precious bag is lost to the darkness. A savage howl escapes his trembling lips, using precious air. Bastard! Bastard! Bastard! Pounds like a murderous mantra in his mind as he kicks his flippers to speed the ascent. His diving computer emits one long, unending beep. The higher he goes, the more the pressure in his suit increases. It will double during the last ten meters of uplift. His thumb manically presses the valve again and again to release pressure and slow the rise, but it's too late. In a whirl of air bubbles, he skyrockets towards the surface.

As Chuck vanishes in the dark depths, Sam gropes for and finds his diving regulator, sticking it in his mouth, taking deep slow breaths. Shining his lamp, he scans the ledge with trembling fingers for his mask, but without luck. He fingers the large thigh pockets on his suit where he hopes to find the extra mask he customarily keeps there. The pockets are empty. No matter. He must calm himself, get his gasping, whistling breath under control. He feels like an astronaut bereft of his ship, drifting in the endless blackness of space. For a moment, panic paralyzes him. He forces his thoughts to one single concept. Up and out, as quickly as possible. Fresh air, discernible reality! Like a forest creature after a shock, he shakes himself knowing that to fight the fear will only encourage it to take hold, escalate to panic and he will die. He must allow his terror to scream while his consciousness focuses on taking one step at a time toward survival. Concentrate!

He squints to decipher the air supply display and has a hazy view of a red light. It's high time he gets to the surface. He controls the rise, trying his damnedest to read the display on his diving device, but the water is too murky. What did they teach him? Do not rise faster than the smallest air bubbles. Those he can see. Breathing as calmly as possible, he fixes his eyes on the bubbles in front of his face, pacing his ascent. It's hard. He is still under shock, his mind and body a tempest of fear and adrenaline. Chuck had seriously intended to kill him! Concentrate! Count! Exhale, twenty-one, twenty-two, twenty-three. Inhale, twenty-one, twenty-two…yes, that's better. He has to control his breath, suspecting he hasn't enough air supply for a three-minute safety stop at five meters' depth. He prays to an unknown entity that he hadn't reached the decompression zone and suffers an embolism upon surfacing. "Breathe, just breathe easy, everything will be fine," he promises himself. He becomes aware of vaguely perceived lights passing over him and vanishing again.

Four minutes later, he surfaces and inflates his vest to the max. Marie and Barbu are heaving Chuck's body over the rim and into the boat. The spotlight is on, bathing the scene in sharp, bright light. Every detail piercing his vision. Sam gathers the rest of his dwindling strength. His legs cramp and he bends double. Panting, he doubts he can propel his weight to the boat. Still, he has to try and weakly paddles the few meters to the circle of light.

"Help me!" Sam calls out from the boat's stern. He's too exhausted to haul himself and his equipment up and is clinging to the aluminum ladder. He unclips his vest and removes his flippers. Barbu's face appears, his eyes wide, his expression confounded. He leans forward wordlessly, scoops his hands under Sam's armpits and heaves him up with a loud grunt. Sam falls belly down over the boat's rim, sliding onto the deck like a tuna fish on a grappling hook. He sees Barbu fishing his vest and tank from the water, dropping them next to him on the deck. Sam's legs are still dangling over the edge of the boat, his arms stretched over his head, trembling. His head turned aside; he sucks in air through compressed lips. He coughs up red mucous and snot is streaming from his nose.

Utterly spent, he is unable to move. His body shudders violently with each exhalation and his mind races through his extremities, looking for initial symptoms of diver's paralysis. Panic rising, he checks for pain in his joints. Can he feel his feet? If the bends were severe, bubbles of dissolved nitrogen in his blood would have already migrated to his joints and nervous system and he would have had an embolism the moment he surfaced. He's not unconscious, so that's a good thing. And he's still alive. His body is quaking, but he feels no piercing pain in his joints. Sam rolls to the side, wiping mucous from his face and inspecting the red snot in his hands. Maybe a small blood vessel in his lungs had burst? If he survives the next few minutes and is symptom free, he's made it. He will survive.

Groaning, he rises up on his elbows and squints down the length of the boat. Marie is bent over Chuck, his head in her hands, talking softly. Barbu is taking a pair of scissors to the tight neck cuff on his neoprene suit. Sam comes to his knees, coughing and spluttering mucous.

Chuck's eyes are extremely distended, gazing up at Marie. He's alive and conscious. Foamy, red blood swells from his mouth that is moving but making no sound.

Barbu is moving like a well-oiled machine. They had all moaned and groaned during their diving rescue and emergency training, actions they were required to repeat a thousand times until they could do them in their sleep. As if on remote control, Barbu grabs the bottle of emergency oxygen, hurriedly attaching the hoses to the valve. He holds the mask over Chuck's nose and mouth, removing it every second or so to flick off blood with his fingers. Barbu's face is expressionless, his entire energy is focused on one goal – to pump oxygen into Chuck's body. Otherwise, Chuck will die. Stroking Chuck's hair, Marie looks up and her eyes find Sam's. Her eyes widen and her jaw drops.

"Mon Dieu!" she gasps, pointing to Sam and then jogging Barbu's shoulder, who looks around at Sam. He looks dreadful! Pale as a corpse, blue nose and lips, a thread of blood dripping from his mouth. Without missing a beat, Barbu snatches up the other mask, hooks it up and reaches it over to Sam.

With the mask to his mouth, Sam concentrates on breathing slowly and rhythmically. For heaven's sake, don't hyperventilate! Pure oxygen will open his blood vessels clogged with toxic bubbles, bringing the life-saving gas to his cells. I'll be fine, I'll be fine, I'll be fine he chants in his mind, stretching each phrase, longer, longer, longest, timing his inhalation and exhalation to each slowly repeated phrase.

He turns his head and finds Chuck's eyes locked on his face. An empty look, but a living one. Then Chuck's eyelids begin to flutter, and a shudder runs through his body. His vision turns to glass, his eyes gyrating uncontrollably and then roll to the back, only the whites showing.

Barbu places his fingers on Chuck's jugular, searching for a pulse. He presses the mask into Marie's hand and kneels over Chuck, first massaging then pumping hard to contract his heart muscle. "one, two, three, four, five, six," he counts out loud. In the pause, Barbu bends over and covers the blood-smeared mouth, blowing a breath of air into Chuck's nose and then resumes pumping his heart. Marie replaces the oxygen mask. Barbu intensifies the pressure of his strokes and Sam hears an ugly cracking in Chuck's ribcage. A broken rib or two is not fatal, but the foamy blood streaming from Chuck's mouth with every new stroke is. Apparently, his lungs are torn. Barbu stops CPR, falling to his side, his bloody hands covering his face.

"Mais non!" Marie cries out, rising up over Chuck to continue reanimation, but Barbu pulls her gently away and holds her tightly in his arms. It's no use. It's over. Chuck is dead.

Sam crawls over to them and lays his arms around Marie from behind her. Her whole being is shaking with sobs. When she feels his touch, she twists away from Barbu and looks Sam in the eyes. What does he see there? Shock? Grief? Rage?

"What on earth happened, Sam?" She pants, her lips trembling, her hands stroking his face. Sam tries to remove the oxygen mask he is still holding over his face, but Marie presses his hand back.

"Jesus Christ!" Barbu moans, righting himself and leaning against the boat's side. His eyes flickering incredulously from Chuck to Sam, from Sam to Chuck.

Sam lifts the oxygen mask and haltingly begins to recount the underwater struggle. After every few words, he has to stop and catch his breath as if he has sprinted five kilometers without a break and his body can't afford to breathe more slowly. He tells them exactly what transpired, only omitting his intention to sink the bag of diamonds.

The story told, Sam sits gasping and presses the oxygen mask back onto his mouth and nose.

Marie takes him in her arms and presses him on her body. Trembling in unison, Sam hears Barbu relate what he had seen on the surface. They were shocked when they saw Chuck's vest rocket from the water without Chuck inside it. They immediately started the motor and turned on the lights. Just after they had heaved the vest and tank on board, Chuck himself shot through the surface. His suit was filled to the max and Chuck looked like the Michelin man. Barbu immediately knew something had gone deadly wrong.

Barbu's words are accompanied by sobs. His brain tries to deny what it has seen and find another explanation. Rewriting history. Yet, it seems human beings can only accept something they can grasp. Only then can they process it. Barbu struggles for clarity, but there is only a haze of incomprehensible events.

Barbu slides over to Chuck's vest and examines it, showing them where the hose to the air tanks had been torn loose. The shoulders had scrape marks and the tank was scored.

"Look here. Evidently, the steel cable attached to that damned bag got tangled up in his equipment. He was probably trying to inflate everything he had to lift himself and the bag to the surface," Barbu speculates.

"It's a wild guess, but I would think he took off the vest to unravel the cable," Sam adds.

"Merde! That can't be! Chuck has more experience than all of us and he would never do anything so stupid! Lose his vest? Ascending without control? It just doesn't sound like him!" Marie insists, holding the vest like some sacred relic. What in God's name really happened down there? What caused this horrible accident? Was the shelf unstable? Did something get entangled in the steel cable? Or was Chuck's equipment defect? Her mind races through a thousand scenarios, looking for solid ground in which she could anchor her grief.

"Whatever happened, we need to think fast, we're getting company," Sam cuts in, pointing to small green and red lights swaying over the water. There is a boat coming their way.

Marie and Barbu follow Sam's finger.

"We need to decide what to do. If they find Chuck's body on board, there will be an investigation. They'll dive and find something down there for sure and the whole nightmare will start all over again," Sam says coldly, shuddering at the prospect.

Barbu looks at him appalled until he understands what Sam is inferring. He nods and begins to take lead weights from the supply box.

"You couldn't possibly!" Marie watches in horror. Sam looks her in the eyes, and she reads his determination. The same grim purpose is on Barbu's face. When she sees just how possible it is for the two men, she turns away, leaning on the boat's rim, her face pressed to her knees. Her entire body is quivering as if she were the one who had just gotten out of the icy water.

Barbu opens the thigh pockets on Chuck's suit, aiming to fill them with lead weights. To his amazement, he finds a baggie full of mid-sized stones on one side and, immediately checking the other, pulls out the bag with the large stone.

"So, Chuck wouldn't do anything so stupid, would he? Here's your proof!" He snorted, tossing the bags at Marie's feet. She lifts the bags and looks at them thoughtfully, but Barbu rips them from her hands again.

"Enough!" He cries softly through pressed lips. "Enough! These damned stones have done enough damage, it has to end!" He looks daggers at Marie and then throws the two bags with all his might far into the lake. With a small splash they vanish.

Marie follows the bags' trajectory with her eyes and when they hit the surface she seems to waken to reality. She jumps up in whirl of activity, helping Sam and Barbu fill Chuck's suit pockets with weights. She stuffs the remaining weights into the vest pockets and presses out the last hiss of air.

Barbu lifts the diving vest over the boat's rim.

"Wait a second," Sam calls softly. He hangs Chuck's flippers, lamp and mask on the carabiners. Barbu nods and lets the vest glide into the water. Then, with united strength, the three of them heave Chuck's strong, stocky body onto the railing. Marie stuffs the small oxygen mask into the suit and kisses Chuck on the cheek.

Barbu and Sam lower the body into the lake, holding him by the feet for a short moment.

"Rest in peace, my friend," Marie whispers, and as if ordered to do so, the two men repeat the last blessing and give his body back to the depths and the sunken stones.

Chuck's body does a slow somersault and sinks quickly, feet first. For a second, his white face appears just beneath the surface, his eyes staring sightlessly up at them. And then his body vanishes into the black depths.

Here, the lake floor lies two hundred and sixty meters below. His body will meet the silky silt which will first enshroud him, then swallow him. A cold grave never touched by the sun. No flowers or engraved marker will tell that someone cares; someone still keeps his memory alive. Should anyone try to retrace his footsteps, they might find that he had traveled to Switzerland. And there, his influence on this life ended. Chuck was thirty-two years old when he died. His life, one long battle to get his foot in the door. To mold with his own hands the shape his life would take. And that had been within reach, if it had been enough. But wealth was not enough. He wanted more, he wanted everything. Here, his wanting ended in the freezing slick, falling deeper and deeper into its engulfment. Maybe his body will fossilize and be found in a hundred thousand years. And should humanity still exist, they might wonder about how he once was dressed or how his body was formed. Maybe they would assume he was a man from outer space, examining the neoprene remnants beneath a microscope, and surmise he had fallen from the sky to his death.

They are still standing at the boat's stern, staring into the water when a spotlight sweeps slowly over the boat, breaking their reverie.

"Are you all right? Do you need help?" a voice calls from behind them. Blinded, they could only vaguely see the shape of two people in the boat pulling up alongside theirs.

Once the spotlight moves out of their vision, Sam recognizes the local police boat. One of the officers comes on board and shines his light in their faces. Sam racks his brain and comes up with a lame excuse. He was diving and his two friends, both foreigners, were helping him. Everything's fine, he explains, he just came up too fast and was a bit woozy, but he thinks he's okay.

The police think it's odd that Sam was diving alone. That's irresponsible, especially at night. What on earth was he diving for by himself? Sam explains that he wanted to take dramatic night photos of the cliff for a diving magazine. He got caught up in taking shots and went too deep. He lost his camera on the ascent, to boot.

The officers shake their heads. That's incredibly foolhardy, diving alone and then at night, too. "What in the world were you thinking?" one of them berates Sam. But when Sam shows them his diving instructor license and they see he is a local, they let up a bit. The world is full of nuts. They know that only too well. Tourists looking for kicks go canyoning and never surface. So why not a diving instructor taking ultimate images of a cliff wall in icy depths, drawing even more kamikaze fools determined to dive here! At least they wouldn't have to scrape them from the wall, like the base jumpers. Divers just disappear, erased from the surface of the Earth, so to speak. Or if they do turn up, then a few days later at one of the lake's beaches. All the police had to do was throw out the fishing net and reel him in, hoping he didn't stink too badly.

All the same, they let it go, at least for the moment. They do insist on escorting Sam to the hospital and that he come to the station tomorrow to make a statement. They want to be on the safe side, just in case this idiot diver dies from the aftereffects of his stupid adventure. Which, from the looks of him, is a possibility. At least they have followed protocol and couldn't be held responsible.

Marie and Barbu chug back toward Sam's house, navigations lights gleaming, while Sam is stowed in the back of the police boat that races full throttle to the hospital in Interlaken.

High above, on the cliff overlooking the lake, a man kneels down to stuff his night vision scope back into his backpack on the ground next to him. He straightens and rubs his burning eyes with one hand, while pulling his anorak zipper up to his chin. Temperatures have dropped since he's been standing there.

He stretches his stiff legs, then swings his backpack over his shoulders and onto his back, rummaging in his coat pocket for his cellphone. Treading softly, he makes his way back to the side road where his car is parked. Twigs snap beneath his soles as he speaks quietly into the phone.

Additional books by Stefan Prebil

Icediamonds Volume 1

WHO FAILS TO HONOR,
WILL BE HUMBLED

Paperback 978-3-7497-9660-1
Hardcover 978-3-7497-9661-8
E-Books   978-3-7497-9662-5

LORENA – 2032 Die Zeit der
Wahrheit

Paperback ISBN: 978-3-7497-2629-5
Hardcover ISBN: 978-3-7497-2650-9
e-Book ISBN: 978-3-7497-2651-6
Hörbuch: ISBN 978-3-033-06774-5

English Version in 2020

Zeitfracht Medien GmbH
Ferdinand-Jühlke-Straße 7
99095 Erfurt, Deutschland
produktsicherheit@kolibri360.de